We Are Ghost Lit

WE ARE GHOST LIT

A NOVEL

JAMES BRUBAKER

Though portions of this novel were inspired by real events, this is a work of fiction. Any similarity to real persons is coincidental and not intended by the author.

FIRST EDITION, August 2023

ISBN 10: 8985725650
ISBN 13: 9798985725650

Book design by Savannah Adams

Braddock Avenue Books
P.O. Box 502
Braddock, PA 15104

www.braddockavenuebooks.com

Braddock Avenue Books is distributed by Small Press Distribution.

I've always known I'll die alone

— James Tiberius Kirk
Star Trek V: The Final Frontier

Row, row, row your boat
Gently down the stream
Merrily, Merrily, Merrily, Merrily
Life is but a dream

— James Tiberius Kirk and Leonard "Bones" McCoy
Star Trek V: The Final Frontier

Life is not a dream

— Spock
Star Trek V: The Final Frontier

More than anything else, Star Trek V is a work of profound ego . . .Shatner can't help but make himself the Star Of The Show in every scene of his movie.

— Jacob Hell
"William Shatner 'Apologizes' for 'Star Trek V: The Final Frontier.' Published on slashfilm.com

WE ARE GHOST LIT

A NOVEL

JAMES BRUBAKER

THE STARMAN IS BORN

and stares into the cosmos surrounding him. How strange, he thinks, to be surrounded by stars when one is—he examines his form—yes, when one is made of stars. This is the Starman's first moment of existence, and it is every moment of all existence. As his conscious thoughts take shape, he is overwhelmed by the sudden flood of information. He is drowning in the history and future of the universe, in all that will exist for *all of time*. He sees the universe around him at its very youngest, and, too, sees it dying—maybe. The Starman can't tell, for sure, if he can see the end of the universe or not—this information, it's all too much. There is too much everything everywhere around him to make sense of anything. And so the Starman concentrates on a cluster of stars that he knows is the Milky Way, then focuses on a time before the Milky Way is formed, when it is just a cluster of stars. Eventually, he unfocuses his attention, sees a centillion or more Milky Ways, one for every moment in which the Milky Way exists. The Starman thinks about how many stars he is looking at, stars upon stars upon stars, multiplied by all of time. His vision blurs, his head throbs, he vomits stardust then cries out in anguish.

"What is troubling you, Starman?" The voice booms inside the Starman's head, but is difficult to discern because he can hear every conversation he will ever have.

He tries to speak but makes no sound. He is trying to say, "It's too much."

The voice says, "I know it is a lot."

The Starman focuses on the sound of the voice, somewhat isolating it from the mess of sound in his head, tries to listen to the specific moment that this particular voice is talking to him. As he regains his composure, he realizes he can't speak because there is nothing in space to carry sound. He says without saying, "You are the Universe?" He waits for an answer though he knows it to be true because he already exists in the moment the Universe answers, and all the moments after that.

The Universe says, "I am."

The Starman says, "You are cruel. I know not to trust you."

"That's probably smart."

"I'm not sure why. I can't see through all the clutter." Then, "I don't want this."

"What do you mean you don't want this?"

"I don't want to see all of time, all of the time."

"You are the Starman. This is part of what you are."

"But I'm already exhausted."

"You will get used to it."

"But what am I? If I exist in all of time at once, shouldn't I at least know that?"

The Starman focuses his attention and looks for his origin, but he cannot see it because from the moment he was born, he always was. It's a strange paradox—he remembers waking up for the first time having *always already existed*. This confuses the Starman when he thinks about it. He isn't even sure if this conversation with the Universe is right after when he was born, or at some other point in time.

"Have faith, Starman."

"Why am I here?"

"Does it matter?" the Universe says.

The Starman says, "Why won't you help me?"

"I help only those who help themselves."

The Starman, frustrated and even more exhausted, says, "I think I need to rest now, close my eyes for a little while."

The Universe says, "You do that. I'm not going anywhere."

And with that, the Starman closes his eyes, sticks his fingers in his ears, and sets himself adrift through space.

Let him rest. There's no hurry. And anyway, before long the Starman will learn that, though he will still *exist*, will *always* exist in all of time, his consciousness can easily slip into temporal linearity at any point on the timeline, and exist as mortal beings do. This will take only a thought from the Starman, like flipping a switch, and so he can also exit linear time and return to experiencing all of time at once. Because he doesn't have anything else to do, and is naturally curious, the Starman will enter the linear flow of time early in the Universe's history, and will spend his days, months, years, decades, centuries, millennia, eons, wandering the cosmos. He will periodically be scolded by the Universe for refusing a gift so mighty as knowing all of time at once, yet the Starman will persist. He will explore solar systems and galaxies. He will sit at planets—our own, Earth, among them—for thousands of years just to watch life develop, and then to watch that life form tribes, villages, cities, countries. He will come to appreciate watching lifeforms develop communities, to care for and take care of one another. He will wonder what it is like to comfort a loved one with a hug. He will wonder what it feels like to kiss, be kissed, to make love. He will marvel at the grandeur of the Universe, and be a little bit grateful that he came to exist in a way that he might enjoy the splendor surrounding him—but only a little bit, because he will also begin to feel immensely alone. After all, with whom can a starman build a community? The Universe is not good company, and it's not like the Starman can rearrange the stars to make another Starman (or Starwoman). He knows—he's tried. He will encounter comets, black holes, quasars, and other cosmic entities with which he can *almost* communicate, but not quite. Sometimes the Starman will slide momentarily back into nonlinear time, thinking that maybe he can drown out the lonely feelings with sensory overload, or perhaps even answer his loneliness by arriving at a better understanding of what he is, where he came from, why he exists—if he could just understand what it's all *for*, the Starman supposes, perhaps he would be able to live with his loneliness. The Starman will not find the answers he seeks. He will find something else, though. Approximately thirteen billion years into his travels through the Universe, the Starman will encounter a human. The first time the Starman sees the human, he will be alone, reading a large book—a book about the stars, even—under a tree. The human, who is young at the time of this first observation, will appear content. The Starman will envy that contentedness, and for no other conscious reason be drawn to this Earth Boy, will take a special interest in him. He will try to befriend him. Eventually, the Earth Boy will grow less content, and the Starman will try to help him by helping himself. *This* will be the defining story of the Starman's existence. The Starman will recognize the strangeness of a cosmic entity being so fascinated by a human, but that fascination will make the Starman feel less alone, at least for a little while, and that's good for something.

This is the story I will be telling, though I am not the only narrator in this novel. The other narrators will tell different stories, stories more important, perhaps, to the novel's goals. If the other stories are more important, one might ask, why are we starting here, with this brief, unofficial preface? We start here because the Starman is damn near infinite, and by existing in all of time, he existed billions of years before those other narrators' stories take place. If that's not good enough reason, I don't know what is.

PART ONE

ALPHA AND OMEGA

The first time I met you, we were in elementary school and you were dressed as Spock for Halloween. You weren't dressed like Spock in Starfleet, though—no blue science officer shirt or red naval uniform—you were dressed in a white robe and matching headband, the way Spock dressed after he died in *The Wrath of Khan* and was resurrected, in *The Search for Spock,* by his friends who loved him too much to let him stay dead. We're talking Spock in *Star Trek IV: The Voyage Home*, here, the one where he and the rest of the Enterprise crew travel back in time so that they can bring two humpback whales to the future, so Spock tears a strip of fabric from his robe and wears it as a headband to hide his pointy Vulcan ears from the humans of San Francisco in 1986. It's a convoluted story, but it's fun. It's also somewhat haunting when we start to unpack the underlying context of the film's plot—here: in the movie's vision of the future, Earth's humpback whales have gone extinct and somewhere across the universe, in some dark corner unexplored by Starfleet, an alien race had been communicating with said whales using the mammals' songs. Then, suddenly, when there were no whales left to sing those songs that once traversed the silent husk of space, the aliens sent a probe to find out why their friends had gone silent. Maybe the aliens thought they'd done something wrong. Perhaps one of them asked aloud, "Were we asking too much?" So they sent a probe that arrived hundreds of years too late, because the whales died long before their final songs could reach those mysterious aliens. Long story short—the probe unintentionally destroys Earth, because that's what probes sent by mysterious aliens do, meaning the Enterprise crew, including the newly-back-from-the-dead Spock, have to travel to the past and bring two humpback whales into the future—their present—to converse with the probe and repopulate Earth's oceans with the species, thus saving Earth and its people. It's a nice idea, bringing an extinct species back from the dead. It's almost as nice an idea as distant aliens listening to whale song across millions or billions or trillions of miles. Of course, in the movie we never see the aliens, just their probe, which is a giant, black cylinder with a protrusion, a glowing orb like a sci-fi disco ball. Maybe the aliens were whales, too—whales who could build probes and travel through space.

But fuck.

We're not here to talk about *Star Trek IV: The Voyage Home*. We're here to talk about *you*, whom I met when you were in fifth and I was in fourth grade, when you dressed as Spock for Halloween and I dressed like Sherlock Holmes, wearing an ill-fitting suit, and one of my dad's raincoats. On my head I wore two ball caps turned opposite directions and painted brown, and in my mouth I held something made from a flexi-straw and the bottom of a Dixie cup, glued together to almost resemble a pipe. And when we met, I said, "I like your costume," and you said, "I like your costume," and then we were friends for thirty years and then you were gone.

The last time I saw you was right after Christmas 2014. You were drunk. I drove you home to your father's house, where you were staying while in town from London for the week. You'd lived across the pond, as you liked to say, for more than a decade, having taken a job there after finishing your bachelor's degree in the States. In the car that night, you spoke of loneliness and love. You said, "There are women who I've loved and now they're married and have kids, and where am I? What do I have to show for my life?" And I said, "You have a career, and you are strong, and you have a heart as big as some astrophysicists' conception of space-time that sings like a single trumpet holding a high C for a split second after the rest of the band cuts off." You said, "But what do I have to *show* for it?" In your words, I heard how truly hollow space-time can be. I heard the silence that follows after the trumpeter rips the horn from his lips. I thought about that trumpet player and the way we hear his note, pure and powerful, for just a second, maybe less, and then it's gone.

[A confession: I didn't really say that thing to my dead friend that I wrote that I'd said in the previous section. I mean, I wish I'd said that, and what I actually *did* say was basically the same thing, probably. That is, I'm sure I said something like, "You have a lot to show—a great job and you're a really fantastic person." And then I probably said something stupid to be funny, and not make the moment feel *too* sincere, something like, "And you've got a massive dong—you'll find someone." And then my dead friend probably said something like, "Maybe," which, looking back, probably meant, "Everything's bullshit. It doesn't really matter, anyway." But trying to reimagine that moment now, through the lens of the present, is impractical, a waste of time. Were I to read such resignation in my dead friend's "maybe," now, I'd be assuming that he somehow knew he was going to die, which I don't believe to be the case, I don't think. Why would I believe that? Because of some shit he said when he was drunk nine months before he died? Because, to be honest, in retrospect, he seemed to be drifting away, slowly untethering himself from those who loved him in the final months of his life? Because of a specific message he sent, which didn't mean much when received, but which I've since completely avoided thinking about after I learned that he'd died? Why would any of that make me think my dead friend knew he was going to die? Or that, perhaps, he'd even do something so outlandish as take his own life? It's all too easy to try to turn moments into clues, to try to add it all up so that it becomes something it isn't. That's all beside the point, though. For now, I'm just going to think about how I regret saying something so banal and making that bad joke when I could have said something with actual substance.

But really, it's ok that I didn't say the thing that I wrote I had said. This isn't a memoir, exactly. Or it isn't a memoir at all. No, this is a work of fiction. And the James Brubaker narrating this book outside of the brackets isn't me, or is maybe a better version of me, or a lesser version, or maybe is altogether a stranger, someone I have never met, and who I wouldn't recognize if I saw him in public. That other James Brubaker, he is a construction, let's say. How Borgesian, I know. Perhaps if I *did* encounter this other me on the street, I would recognize myself in his features, his build, perhaps even his mannerisms, but the moment he opened his mouth, I'd recognize him as untrue. So, why don't I write him true? Why not make him me? Maybe I'm simply acknowledging that identity, like narrators, is constructed to mediate the gaps between stimuli and sensation, thought and communication, the real Truths that are lost between how something feels and the words we're stuck with to describe that feeling. Or maybe I find comfort in hiding behind a constructed avatar. Maybe I'm afraid.]

The first thing I did when I heard you were gone? I drove to the store, bought a pack of smokes. No, the first thing I did when I heard you were gone: I bought a pack of Camels, even though I'd been more or less quit for years, and I drove down to the river. No, the first thing I did when I heard you were gone: I tried not to cry until I hung up the phone. No, the first thing I did when I heard you were gone was to go down to the river and look up at the sky, at the stars, and remember, at first, not a photo you once took and shared on social media of Sagittarius A*, but another picture that accompanied it, a picture of the beach at night, the spot where you sat to take the more impressive photo—your camera set on a tripod, tilted upward to see the sky, the empty chair beside it. That empty chair where you'd sat. No, the first thing I did when I heard you were gone was to look at the last text message you'd sent me months before your death and decide, then and there, not to look at it again, ever, not to think about it. No, the first thing I did when I heard you were gone was ask—how? No, the first thing I did when I heard you were gone was ask—why?

And that's a perfectly natural way to react, especially upon learning of a death so unexpected, and of someone so close. Wrapped in the weight of that *why* was the entire history of our friendship—the way we used to sing "Swinging on a Star" while driving around Dayton, Ohio, where we lived, not because we really liked the song, well, you did, maybe, but because we liked the way it was used in *Hudson Hawk,* which was, otherwise, a pretty bad movie; the time you gave me my first cigarette, my first semester at college—though I didn't choose my college because you were already attending, it *was* helpful to start there with at least one friend—and told me not to smoke it because smoking is terrible, but you knew I was hurting because I was dating a girl back home, and it wasn't going well—we broke up then, but reunited sixteen years later and are married now, I call her B., not her name, or even an initial, it's just a thing we do—so I was determined to smoke a goddamn cigarette, and you let me, and then you taught me how not to take it straight into my lungs, but to draw the smoke into my mouth first, then inhale it; and the time another friend stole what turned out to be a handmade baby Jesus from a nativity scene, lovingly set out in front of a private residence in the rural outskirts of Bowling Green, Ohio, and you felt so bad about it that we drove the pitch-black country roads for four hours—having to stop for gas once, even—searching for the house our friend had taken it from just so we could return it, but we never found the house; or the time that, after learning that one of your high school crushes was going on a date with another of your friends, we—meaning you, me, and a couple of other guys, and our friend Parker, who always wound up hanging out with the guys, even when the other girls in our friend group were having sleepovers, or watching movies together—went to the Little League field near your house after dark with a traffic cone and an M-80 firecracker, which we believed at the time was as powerful as a quarter stick of dynamite, though we later learned that wasn't true, and you lit the M-80 and dropped it in the hole at the top of the traffic cone, and you ran away, and turned around where the rest of us were standing, just in time to see the cone fly through the air, glide in front of the moon and so many stars, and come spiraling back down, landing blackened and frayed a few feet away from us; or the time another old friend from junior high, whom neither of us had talked to in years, died suddenly—from a brain aneurysm—and so we sipped beers on the front stoop of your apartment, a two-story townhouse for college kids, surrounded in rows by identical townhouses, and chainsmoked cigarettes, and you said, "I kept meaning to call him, or email him, but I kept putting it off because I thought I was too busy," and I said, "And he could be kind of exhausting to talk to, after Shannon left him." You said, "That too." And I said, "I hadn't talked to him in two years—why does it feel so strange knowing he's gone?" And you said, "Because he can't answer the phone now, even if we tried."

I understand that more, now.

After I heard you were gone, I couldn't quite make sense of a world without you in it, a world where you wouldn't be able to answer the phone, even if I tried. Though for more than a decade we'd seen each other only once a year, sometimes every other year, our old rhythms returned easily when we were reunited—as if no time had been lost between us, as if you were never really away at all. Now, I'm left with only pieces. What do I remember? You played the trumpet as long as I knew you, and loved to play those high notes, hold them over for half a beat after the rest of the band stopped playing, like Maynard Ferguson. You loved all things Star Trek. You made friends easily, and kept them almost as easily. You liked to play games, computer and tabletop. You loved the stars and anything having to do with space—while at college, you worked part-time at the planetarium on campus, showing visitors the stars through a telescope. You even invented a being you referred to as the Starman, who lived in space and was made up of stars, but also moved among the stars, and turned out to actually be real. You were happy and easygoing, but also contained inside you a profound sadness. You may or may not have been catfished once. Despite being loved by so many, you were one of the loneliest people I've ever known. And now you're dead. That's what I'm left with. That and a deep, impenetrable grief. Sometimes I think I'm incapable of working through that grief, but maybe, really I'm more worried that if I ever successfully work through it I won't remember you at all.

One thing I can never remember about you because I never knew it to begin with: how you died. I know that your body was found in a hotel room. I know that we were given different sets of facts about your death, one by each of your parents, and another by your brother. I understand that I will probably never know how you died. I think about this a lot—try to piece it all together, to understand how and why it happened. Really, though, I recognize that this is just another way for me to keep you present in my thoughts just a little while longer.

[In case it isn't obvious: I'm writing this novel on the other side of loss. How does one write about loss? About grief? I used to write stories about imagined loss—what it would be like to lose someone. I wrote stories about how it might feel to lose a father, a wife. Specifically, my father, my now ex-wife. The loss I'm setting out to write about, here, is that of a friend. He was thirty-six when he died. I saw him at Christmas when he was in town from London visiting family, and then I never saw him again. In the nine months between our last meeting and his death, we exchanged a few emails, commented on each other's social media posts, he sent me a text message—and then he was gone. Dead. Over. I will never see him again. No one will ever see him again. It's *that* loss, *that* absence I'm writing through, here. When I wrote those old stories about losing my father and my wife who isn't my wife anymore, I know, now, that I was learning how to say goodbye. So maybe by writing this, whatever it is that I'm writing, I can learn how to say goodbye to my dead friend.]

IF WE CAN SPARKLE HE MAY LAND TONIGHT

Right now, let's talk about the stars, because you had a profound interest in space, would spend nights looking through telescopes, taking pictures of the sky. You looked for and named new constellations—when you were younger, the names were after songs by Tangerine Dream and the cities in or around where you'd lived; when you were older, the names were taken from "the loves you'd let slip through your fingers," your words, not mine. After you'd show me a constellation, I'd be struck by how much it looked like the named thing. You connected dots in the shapes of cities and faces. You couldn't make the stars look like a song, so those constellations were interpretations of the songs' titles: for "Sequent 'C,'" three letter Cs in succession; for "Thru Metamorphic Rocks," the stars formed an impressively detailed banded rock, "Like slate," you'd say, "or gneiss"; for "Invisible Limits," the constellation was the entire sky; and for "3:00 a.m. at the Border of the Marsh from Okefenokee," the stars formed the swamp of the song's name, rendered in vivid detail with small sets of stars shaped into Sun Dew and Bladdermort, into an alligator's head lifting up from the gently rippling water, into an osprey tending its nest. When I asked how we knew it was 3:00 a.m., you said, "It's 3:00 a.m. everywhere, forever between the stars." I couldn't argue with that. Once, at college, we sat out smoking and drinking in a field by the dorms and I watched you devise a new constellation: "There, close to the horizon, that star is a foot; and there, up from it a bit?—that's a hand. Those three stars in a line—not Orion's belt—her smile." Here, I asked who you were making. You ignored my question, continued mapping the form in the sky above us, the chin, the curve of a cheek, the eyes, shoulders, neck, clavicle, and then you said, "And there, straight below the smile, see that star like a whispering mouth?" I told you I saw it. Then you said, "You know." I knew, but I didn't say anything even though the whispering mouth metaphor was terrible and gross. Then you said, "This constellation is named Michelle."

I was surprised by the name. I asked, "You've never made a Michelle before?" You said, "I've made a thousand Michelles. Sometimes I feel as if every constellation has been a Michelle." I said, "Oh." And you said, "Exactly."

Later that evening, under the same sky, the same stars, you asked me, "Have you ever seen the Starman?" I said, "The Jeff Bridges movie?" You said, "No, the one in the sky." I laughed at you and said, "Shut the fuck up." But you continued, told me all about this Starman, how he is made of stars connected by stardust, and how he moves between galaxies in search of something—what? You didn't know. Who knows? How could anyone know? I asked, "What the actual fuck are you talking about?" You said, "All I know is this: sometimes I see a starman in the sky but I don't know what he is." Certain, by then, that you were fucking with me, I asked, "Would he like to come to meet us?" You laughed. I said, "Does he think he'd blow our minds?" And this time you were the one who said, "Shut the fuck up," and like you actually meant it, like somehow my making fun of what I thought was you fucking with me actually upset you. Chastised, I looked up at the sky, squinted, pointed, said, "Is that him?" You said, "Don't patronize me." But here's the thing, and I'm not sure you ever believed me, but whether it was because I'd convinced myself out of a desire to be a good friend, or because I actually saw it, in that moment, I thought I might actually have seen something or someone that or who could reasonably be considered at least *a* starman, if not *the* Starman. It wasn't long after that that I saw, and knew that I had seen, *the* Starman for sure. You never believed me about that, either.

[Just to be clear, for my friend, there was never a single, actual Michelle. Or rather, there was a Michelle, and she was a nice young woman with whom my dead friend was periodically infatuated, but for our purposes, here, Michelle is more of an idea. Because the lines between truth and fiction blur so easily, and because I suspect readers who know me, who knew my dead friend, will wonder why they never heard mention of a Michelle or, alternately, try to figure out who Michelle actually was, I want to be absolutely clear about this, about Michelle being a construct, a fictional designation, a symbol of my dead friend's penchant for toxic bouts of unrequited love, and not an actual person. This should be obvious, though, as I've already made clear that this book *is* a work of fiction. Yes, I have a real dead friend, but he is very different from the dead friend in this book. Yes, there are similarities between the two dead friends, and maybe that's this book's biggest sin, writing a fictional version of my dead friend into a fictional version of his life and death. But it's not like writers don't do this all the time, weaving their family and friends into their work, changing names and circumstances, calling it fiction—is that so different from what I'm doing here?]

The first time I knew for sure I'd seen the Starman was September 2000. I was lying in the grass outside of my rental house in Bowling Green, listening to Yo La Tengo's *And Then Nothing Turned Itself Inside-Out* on my Discman—its songs synced to late summer's slow bleed into fall, its cover art, a man standing in front of a house in a quiet suburb at night, looking up into a spotlight projected from the sky, perfect for the eerie sense of wonder that comes with being twenty-one years old, lying alone in the grass, looking up at the stars. I was dozing, drifting in and out of sleep to the gentle bass and warm drones that close out the album's last song, "Night Falls on Hoboken," my eyes fixed on a single bright star—I don't know which one, but had you been there, I'm sure you could have told me—when I saw what appeared to be a small cluster of stars undulating like glitter tossed in the wind. Then I saw those stars move from the single, brighter star on which my eyes were fixed to another star. I squinted and could begin to see the faint outline of an iridescent figure, there, stationary beside the second star. The longer I looked, the more my eyes discerned a form made up of the seemingly chaotic points of light. I saw a head and neck, then two arms, two legs, a mass of smaller stars resembling a torso. I began to feel the acute sense that I wasn't alone. After looking and finding no one near, the hair on my neck bristled and my nerves directed my attention back to the odd figure in the sky—was it him? Was he really there? Surely not. But for a brief moment, I was afraid. Then that fear subsided, replaced by a surprising familiarity and comfort. For several minutes, well past the end of "Night Falls Over Hoboken," I stared up at the Starman, soaking in the warmth of his presence. I remained still until the figure of tiny stars shrunk and disappeared, as if absorbed into the bigger star beside it. When I tried to tell you, you barely acknowledged ever having told me about the Starman in the first place. I'd earned the refusal through my mockery.

But how could I not crack a few jokes after you told me about something so seemingly absurd? How could I not at least reference the Bowie song? It was too perfect, and even if the joke was obvious, and even if the Starman *was* real, I couldn't *not* make it. Oddly, now, I can't think about David Bowie without thinking about you. Both because of the Starman, and, too, because Bowie passed just a few months after you, and when I learned he had died, I wept. Before that, I'd never wept when a celebrity died, not even Leonard Nimoy. I wasn't weeping for Bowie, it was for you. The parallels between you and Bowie were easy. Bowie knew he was dying and, while nearing death, celebrated his life by recording and releasing one of the best albums of his career—found a way to say goodbye. You too seemed to be saying goodbye before you died, as if you somehow knew it was coming. But you weren't sick, and I don't believe that you killed yourself, so how could you have known? Maybe you felt your life winding down? Felt the end of your story drawing near and so managed to check in with the important people in your life one last time, as if it were meticulously planned, though really it wasn't? You came to the States and spent time with us, here. You visited your mother, who had recently moved to Costa Rica. You spent time online posting videos in which you told stories about your college days, answered questions from friends, shared what, in retrospect, seem like highlights from your life. And then in September, your father visited you in London. A few days later, you died. I get it—if someone were inclined to believe that you killed yourself, which I don't, it's easy to see how this might all look like you said goodbye to anyone who mattered and then—

The only real connection between you and Bowie, though, is that you named the Starman after that song of his. You told me that on top of our university's planetarium one fall as we sipped High Life from cans and watched constellations slowly crawl across the sky—one of the few times you spoke of the Starman, plied by the beer, no doubt, after initially telling me about him. When I asked for more information, you put on an old-timey movie voice and said, "He's going to be in pictures," still trying to pass it all off like a joke, even as I insisted that *I'd seen him, too*. Now, outside of a couple of mutual friends, the Starman is my only remaining connection to you. Every time I look up at the night sky, I hope to feel him, or it, or whatever looking back at me.

And about what I said earlier, when I implied that, like Bowie, maybe you somehow knew you were going to die, and so used your final months to say goodbye to your loved ones—maybe you *weren't* saying goodbye. Maybe you never plotted a farewell tour. Maybe that's just the kind of person you were—one who seeks out starmen in the sky, and treats each encounter with loved ones as if it were his last.

Honestly, though, it's not hard to believe that maybe your behavior in your final months was simply an attempt to reaffirm connections that had diminished with time. You were always kind, always cared deeply about your friends. Not long, just a few weeks, really, after the first time you told me about the Starman, you threw a party for your brother's birthday. He came to visit for the weekend and you cooked sausages in a frying pan, then simmered them in marinara, tossed with pasta, and served. That night we drank. And we drank. And we drank so much. I wasn't yet twenty-one, so I was drinking a shitty bottle of white wine that someone bought for me at the State Store, and I drank the entire bottle in fifteen minutes—because what did I know?—and lost track of the night. I remember playing *Dr. Mario* in your neighbor's apartment, and then I remember sitting on the sidewalk out front, and then I remember turning my head to the side and vomiting, and vomiting more, and vomiting more, prompting Parker, who had also moved to Bowling Green for school, to laugh at the mess of barely digested spaghetti and cheap white wine and say, "it's still plateable," which she has repeated for years, every time the story is told. And while I don't look back on what I remember of that night fondly, it wasn't all bad. See, I remember you filling bottles with water to clean up the mess I'd made on the sidewalk, and I remember you helping me up and back to your apartment where you settled me on the sofa. And I remember you checking on me throughout the night, giving me water, making sure I wasn't going to choke on my own puke. I remember thinking, even then, that I didn't deserve such treatment. Just two years prior, while at the end of a night of watching local punk bands play at an American Legion hall, I refused to drive another friend home because he'd been drinking, and he had a reputation for puking any time he drank even a little. He asked me, "How will I get home?" I said, "You should have thought of that." Another friend drove the kid home, and, sure enough, the fucker puked in that other friend's car. At the time, I figured I'd won. But when you were making sure I didn't die on your sofa, I thought about that night and I felt like an asshole. And anyway, here's the point of this digression—I remember waking up the next day and feeling both embarrassed at my actions the night before, and humbled by your kindness and generosity, and then I remember telling you, "I really did see your Starman." You said, "I'm sure you saw a lot of shit last night." And I said, "Not last night, when you told me about him." I said, "What is he?" You said, "He's nothing. A thing I made up." I said, "But I saw him." You said, "You can stop now," then you flinched and said, "What's up?" That was a thing you had started doing around then, after doctors discovered a thing in your brain, the exact nature of which you never really explained. We should probably talk about that.

NOTES ON THE STARMAN (1-4)

1.

After billions of linear years floating through space the Starman still doesn't know much about himself or his purpose. He knows that he is mostly star, and not much man. He doesn't think he was born, but that he was made. Or not even made, exactly—as far as he can tell, he simply *is*. Honestly, though, the Starman doesn't really know that, because he has no idea how he came to exist. He knows only what he is and what he does. To be honest, he barely even knows all that. No, the Starman is an odd thing. The Starman doesn't believe that he has a purpose. One would think that, having spent billions of years traveling the cosmos, the Starman would know more. But he doesn't. Most of the time, as far as anyone can tell, he simply sulks around the Universe feeling sad and lonely and sorry for himself. Ah, the life of the Starman is grim indeed.

*

2.

Here's what the Starman knows:

The Starman knows that when he visits a planet and takes the form of one of its inhabitants he is visiting a planet and taking the form of one of its inhabitants. He knows that when he travels to a distant star and swipes his finger across its surface the way a child scoops a finger full of peanut butter from a jar, he is traveling to a distant star and swiping his finger across its surface the way a child scoops a finger full of peanut butter from a jar. He knows that when he reaches his balled fist through a star's corona, its gasses, liquids, deep into its core and touches the exact center, he is touching something that no mortal being can ever touch. He smears some of it on his face beneath his eyes to block the glare from other stars, then spreads bits of it around in the atmosphere of a nearby planet, putting on a show for any inhabitants—star mist!—then balls the rest into solid matter and flicks it out into the cosmos.

The Starman knows that the Universe is an asshole, and not a very good conversationalist. Aloof is probably the word the Starman would most likely use to describe the Universe if asked. Granted, as lonely as the Starman is, he has little choice but to talk to the Universe as it is the only other sentient being with whom the Starman can truly communicate. The Starman doesn't go out of his way to talk to, and mostly avoids altogether approaching, other cosmic entities—black holes and other spatial anomalies, comets, certain clouds of cosmic dust, etc... etc...—because as far as the Starman can tell, they can't quite make conversation, are more like pets who understand the language of the cosmos and can purposefully transmit limited information, but can't chat the way the Universe does, or, for that matter, interact the way the humans of Earth, or any of the other intelligent species on other planets, interact. As it happens, the Starman is very interested in the humans of Earth. Maybe it's because he is lonely, or maybe it's because he is bored, but he watches them more than any other beings in the Universe. Even when he visits Earth and takes the form of a human, the Starman doesn't interact much because he isn't confident in his abilities to emulate the way humans talk to each other. After billions of years spent mostly alone, the Starman is something of an introvert. Is it any wonder he is so lonely?

*

3.

The Starman watched the dinosaurs on Earth, and he also watched the Neanderthals; he was sad when both went extinct. On another planet, far away from Earth, he watched a species like dinosaurs that didn't go extinct, and a species like Neanderthals that didn't go extinct. The species like Neanderthals domesticated the dinosaurs and rode them like humans ride horses, used them as war machines to fight against rival tribes. At least, until the dinosaurs united and turned on their masters. The species like Neanderthals survived, but many of them were eaten. While this was amusing for the Starman to watch, he preferred watching life on Earth. He watched Asutralopithecus afarensis become Homo habilis become Homo erectus become Homo sapiens neanderthelansis become Homo sapiens sapiens, or something like that. He watched humans when they were nomadic, then watched as they settled into communities. He watched, and watched, and watches—it is during all of this watching that he sees the lonely Earth Boy reading a book about stars, and decides that he'd like to befriend him. There is no good reason for this desire. Nor is there a reason why this boy, reading this book, should be of particular interest to the Starman, who has seen billions of other life-forms reading or otherwise engaged in solitary activities—but he's never once been drawn to one the way he is drawn to this specific Earth Boy. Of course, this is many, many, many years after humans as we know them came to be. This is after the Stone Age, the Bronze Age, the Iron Age, the Industrial Revolution, the Machine Age. This is somewhere decades into the Atomic Age, or the Space Age, or the Information Age, or the whatever-the-fuck-it-is age—the Starman can't quite explain it, but something about that boy makes him feel as if all those ages, all of human history, were designed to bring that boy into existence *for the Starman*. Something about this human makes the Starman feel less alone.

*

4.

The Starman recognizes the absurdity of his fascination with the Earth Boy. Why this boy, at this point in history? He's just a child. The Starman wonders if it isn't the boy so much as it is the timing of seeing the boy: After billions of years alone, could it be that seeing another lonely being triggered an empathetic reaction and caused the Starman to feel a kinship with the boy? Perhaps part of what draws the Starman to the Earth Boy is that, despite appearing lonely, the Earth Boy also seems content. Maybe the Starman thinks he could learn something from the human. If the Starman were human, the whole ordeal might be the sort of thing he could chalk up to low blood sugar, or having had a difficult day at the office, but neither of those applies to the Starman. Whatever the reason, the Starman is now focusing his attention primarily on watching the Earth Boy. He watches the human play video games, alone in the basement of his parents' house. He watches the human play baseball in a park with friends. The Starman notes that the boy isn't very good at baseball, and that even when he is with friends, he sometimes acts as if he is alone, kicking the heads off of dandelions in right field, reading magazines about computers while his friends play games. This endears the Earth Boy to the Starman even more. He watches the human draw pictures in sketchbooks, and look up at the stars, and play the trumpet, and go to school.

Abruptly, one day, the Universe says, "What are you doing, Starman?"

The Starman says, "I'm watching a human on Earth. I might like to visit him."

The Universe asks, "Who?"

"A human on Earth. A child. A boy."

"What boy?"

"I saw him on Earth, reading a book. I've never visited a specific person before."

The Universe says, "It's best not to get involved with humans. With any life-forms, really." The Universe goes on to explain that it's ok to visit, like a tourist, but there's no sense getting attached. "No human could possibly understand you," the Universe says. "And anyway, they die so quickly. You'd see all this for yourself if you'd step out of linear time and try to understand the full arc of existence."

The Starman asks, "Do you ever wonder what mortality is like?"

The Universe says, "No."

"They experience so much—they touch each other, comfort each other. They kiss and hug. My stars can't touch anything, really."

"Your stars are always touching me. You are a part of me."

"Have you ever wondered what it's like to have a pleasant conversation, with the wind rustling the leaves around you?"

"This is a waste of time. You shouldn't concern yourself with this human."

The Starman says, "Ah, you're probably right." He doesn't really mean this, but doesn't want to keep justifying himself to the Universe, and anyway, maybe the Universe *is* right. The Starman doesn't want the Universe to be right, but what is there really to gain by watching or visiting a human?

The Universe says, "And anyway, you have all that I contain, all that *I am*, to explore and enjoy."

The Starman says, "What's to enjoy?"

"The call of the cosmos, Starman. The feel of dark matter on your stars, the infinite silence, the delicate glow of celestial bodies."

The Starman says, "Sure." Then he uses a passing meteor to push off and lets himself drift deep into space, away from Earth, and the human, and even though he can't escape the Universe, he at least has left the location of that particular conversation, which is the best he can ever hope for.

THE THING IN YOUR HEAD

During your first year away at college, doctors found a thing in your head. I'm not sure why they were even looking—you'd been feeling funny, or having headaches, or couldn't sleep. All I know is they found something. This all developed for me via long distance, mostly over the year when you'd already gone off to college and I was still a senior in high school. You weren't the first of our friends to be diagnosed with a thing in his head around that time, and so sometimes it's difficult to remember the different things in various people's heads.

Parker, the young woman who *still* likes to talk about my vomit being plateable, had crashed her car earlier that same year. When they took her to the hospital, doctors found a thing in her head, too. There were surgeries and recoveries. She gained weight from the steroids, then lost it all. The thing in her head was still there, but she seemed fine. I didn't think much of it until I moved to Bowling Green and ran into her older brother, Gary, at a party—yes, many people from our high school wound up at Bowling Green. We were in the basement of the rental house where he lived.

He was sipping a can of Natty Light, sitting on a dingy couch surrounded by woozy freshmen. He said, "Brubaker, you need to look out for my sister." I said, "She can take care of herself." He said, "She will die soon if she doesn't clean up her act." Parker loved her cigarettes and gin, didn't and was probably never going to clean up her act, not at that age, and I knew she wouldn't listen to anyone who might try to convince her otherwise. I told Gary I'd try, but I knew I wouldn't. He said, "You have to promise, you can never tell her that we had this conversation." I promised. And then I carried around with me for years the belief that one of my best friends could drop dead at any minute from the thing in her head, unable to even talk to her about it. When, five or six years later, we finally did talk about it, Parker told me she was never in any immediate danger, not after the surgeries, anyway. I still haven't forgotten Parker's older brother and what he told me. I wonder if he was lying to get me to try to convince his sister to stop smoking and drinking, or if his concern was real. But what am I doing here—you know, or knew, all of this. Here's something you couldn't have known because it didn't happen until after you were gone. That thing in Parker's head? It started causing problems again recently, is more or less inoperable, is probably going to require chemo or some experimental treatment. She realized something wasn't right, this time, because her hand started shaking. Doctors told her years ago if her body wasn't working right, make a call, go to a specialist. And so she did. The thing in her head, they call it a diffuse astrocytoma. It sounds lovely, like it has something to do with the stars. Maybe that's what you had in your head? It would have been a fitting name.

But no, the thing in *your* head was different. It was never going to kill you, that was never even a thought—was just a thing that doctors wanted to keep an eye on. So, of course, you decided to have a little fun with it. Before anyone, even you, really understood what the thing was, but after enough of your college friends knew that it existed, you decided to fuck with everyone—the story goes like this: You spent a day complaining about headaches, coolly, casually, yes, even cruelly. To hear you tell it, you paced the complaints beautifully—a brief mention here, a pained look there when you noticed someone's eyes on you. You asked a friend in the dorm room next door for some ibuprofen. You asked people in the hall to keep their voices down—*you went for it*. I wonder what your friends' faces must have looked like later in the day, first as you grabbed your head and screamed in agony, and then when your screams turned to laughter and you looked up at them with wild eyes—just in time to prevent a 911 call—and they realized you were just playing an awful joke. I wonder how I would have felt being in that room and watching you fake something like your own death instead of just hearing about it secondhand. I don't think it would have fazed me at the time—you were going to live forever. *All of us* were going to live forever. And anyway, it was funny as hell.

A year or two after learning about the thing in your head, you began to sometimes twitch. It wasn't an always thing—just occasionally, sometimes three or four times a day, sometimes once every other month. These twitches looked like shivers, like a slight exaggeration of a chill running down a spine—your head would snap to the side and its motion would seem to reverberate through your entire body with a surprising abruptness. Self-conscious as you were, every time you twitched in the company of another person, you'd say, "What's up?" At first, I understood this as a way to dispel embarrassment. Over time, though, the "What's up?" became something else, a part of the twitch itself, a sort of ritual. The phrase was no longer an apology, became a poem or prayer instead, a beautiful addendum to your body's unsolicited movement. You were no longer protecting your pride, you were anointing the moment, bestowing upon anyone in your presence a blessing. I remember with each twitch waiting for the "What's up?", unable to carry on the conversation or take another step or sip of coffee until I heard those words.

"What's up?"

[The thing in my dead friend's head—that was real. It was so real that when my mother called to tell me that my friend had died, my first thought was that something had happened with the thing in his head, that it had grown, or popped, or mixed poorly with booze and antidepressants, or come to life and chewed his body into one big lump of gristle. None of that turned out to be the case, though—no, my dead friend's death had nothing to do with the thing in his head, whatever it was.

Sometimes, I wish it *had* been the thing in his head that killed my dead friend. Another true thing that my experience has in common with the version of the narrator outside of the brackets is that I have no clue how my dead friend died, and suspect I never will. Each of my dead friend's parents, and then his brother, all told different stories, all vague and noncommittal. Maybe it was suicide. Or maybe it was an accidental overdose. Or maybe foul play was suspected. Years later, as you'll soon learn the version of me outside the brackets is doing, I still routinely search the internet looking for the truth. I never find anything. I suspect this will always be something of a mystery. It's not like I can just call up one of his parents and say, "Hey, tell me about the single most painful thing you've ever confronted in your life. Don't leave anything to the imagination."

Of course, that's not so different from what I'm doing with this novel. I don't want this book to hurt anyone or make anyone uncomfortable; I have no desire to split and gut anyone for my creative pursuits. Does this novel have the potential to do that? I don't *think* so. I hope not. But then, I've never known a loss as great as a parent losing a child. I worry that I'm not the best person to weigh this novel's benefits against its potential emotional costs.]

NOTES ON THE STARMAN (5)

5.

For several Earth years, the Starman largely keeps from checking in on the Earth Boy. When he does, though, he notices that as the human grows older, he seems less content with being alone. The human's face begins to look tired, even when it is smiling. There are bags beneath the human's eyes. The Starman grows worried about the human. He wishes even more that he could visit the human, to try to help the human feel better about himself, but this is not to be, at least for now, with the Universe's words echoing in his memory. And so he decides he will do something else for the human instead.

Far away from Earth, the Starman scoops up a pile of space dust and forms it into a sphere. He digs deep into the fabric of space-time and produces a smidge of dark matter, applies it to the dust like truffle oil. Then he scrapes some dust from his own form and rolls it into the mix. What is the Starman doing? He is making a gift for the human. He squeezes the dust motes and dark matter, presses and pushes and pats until he's left with a tight, tiny ball. The Starman pinches the sphere between his fingers, squints to see it, and wonders aloud, "How might I give this to the human?"

The Universe, having heard the Starman, says, "Still concerning yourself with that human?"

The Starman says, "I'm thinking of giving this to him." He holds out his hand, showing off the tiny speck of tightly bound cosmic material in his palm.

The Universe says, "What's the point?"

The Starman says, "The human seems sad, and I want to do something nice. I want to matter to somebody else. I am an orphan adrift in space. The human seems lonely, and I am lonely, too."

The Universe says, "How maudlin." Then: "I am the Universe in which you live, and to be honest, *mattering to others* is overrated."

After a beat in which neither the Starman nor the Universe speaks, the Universe says, "How are you thinking of giving this to the human?"

The Starman looks at the thing again, squints. Rolls it around his palm a little, then presses it to the tip of his tongue to taste it.

The Universe says, "Disgusting."

The Starman ignores this judgment and begins to squeeze the ball again, making it smaller, smaller, smaller still. When it is as small as possible, the Starman holds it up to his eye for one last examination—the ball is virtually invisible.

He says, "I will put it inside his head. Maybe he won't ever even know that he carries a tiny piece of space inside of him, but it will be his. Unless you object?"

The Universe sighs, says, "It is not a question of whether or not I object. You will do as you please. From my vantage point, the object in your hand doesn't yet exist, exists in your hand, and has already been placed inside the human's head. Nothing I say will stop you, and that's fine, because it is a part of time as it has always been, and will always exist until I am gone."

The Starman says, "I'm surprised."

"You wouldn't be if you chose to understand time nonlinearly. You could understand so much."

"I don't want to live like that."

Then the Starman returns to Earth and finds the human, who is older now, a teenager. The Starman hadn't thought he'd been gone from Earth for so long. It must have been what, a few Earth years? That isn't very long at all for the Starman. The human is sitting alone at a computer. The Starman waits for the human to go to sleep, forms a tendril of gas from his stars, reaches down, and slides the small ball of cosmic dust, dark matter, and bits of himself into the human's head, deep inside his brain.

*

PART TWO

THERE WILL BE NO ANSWERS

Three months before you were gone, you visited your mother in Costa Rica. At night you'd visit the beach to take pictures of the stars. You took a tripod, a camera, a chair. You took three trips over two nights, one of them the summer solstice. Among those trips, you spent at least ten hours looking at the sky. You were particularly proud of one of the photos that you took, so you posted it to social media—it's still there, I look at it frequently. You said that the photo was of the constellation Sagittarius at the center of the Milky Way. You explained that deep inside there is an astronomical radio source called Sagittarius A*, a supermassive black hole around which our solar system revolves. The photograph was stunning, like the cover of a textbook or something hanging on a wall in a planetarium; there was the black of space, hueing purple, bleeding into the brilliant burst of stars at the photograph's center, which spiraled out from a core both dark and light at once—Sagittarius A*, the black hole at the center of the Milky Way.

I tried for a long time to find meaning in all of this. I wondered, were you looking for the Starman? Were you communing with him? Seeking answers from him the way I scoured your old social media posts after you died? Or were you simply marveling at how it feels to be orbiting a supermassive black hole? It was after that trip that you sent me the message that I'm not going to talk about, that I'm not going to think about.

Maybe you set out to photograph Sagittarius A* because it was something you'd always wanted to do, and you knew you were going to die. But that supposes you knew you were going to die, and I don't, can't believe that. Forget about the message you sent. Forget about the way you seemed to be saying goodbye to everyone you loved. Forget the fact that the first news any of us heard of your passing was that you'd killed yourself. It all sounds so easy, but it's not—there's nuance here. The evidence is all circumstantial. The pieces don't quite add up.

And that's why I've concluded that there is a mystery here. Your mother told us suicide, your father said accidental overdose, and then your brother told us you were found in a cheap hotel room, that investigators seized your computer. The simple fact that there were investigators seemed important. I hoped that would go somewhere, that something so formal as an official investigation might produce a trail I might follow to the truth of your demise. For years after your death, I'd type "[Your Name] +death +London" into Google, looking for police reports, articles about mysterious deaths, maybe an obituary. I found nothing. I began to concoct stories about what really happened:

You were drugged at a bar and led to a hotel where you were robbed. The drugs were too much for your body, and the thieves left you to die because they were afraid they'd be caught if they called for an ambulance.

Or in a fit of loneliness, you arranged to meet an escort, who, as it happens, wasn't really an escort but a woman and a couple of guys—or maybe it was just the guys—who pulled you into the room where you'd arranged to meet, drugged you, and robbed you. This story ends like the first.

Or you were catfished. You met a woman online who seemed kind and caring. You spent months getting to know her, and then it was finally time for the two of you to meet. Maybe she was married and decided, she told you, that she would end her marriage—could you just meet her at this hotel so she can *know* you're worth the risk? And then *she* ended up being a couple of guys looking for money. They took you to an ATM at gunpoint, made you withdraw your daily limit, then they took you back to the hotel where they drugged you, resulting, intentionally or not, in your death. Or maybe they just killed you outright and took your wallet.

Or you were a victim of corporate espionage. A rival web design firm thought you were too good at your job, or maybe you knew too much about their design strategies, or you knew they were engaged in unethical behavior, or maybe they tried to poach you only to be rebuffed, and so they hired thugs to dose and murder you.

Or you, tired and frustrated, staying at a hotel for some reason, perhaps because you were too drunk to get home, looked out the window, up at the sky, and begged the Starman to come and get you. When he arrived, your fragile human brain exploded from meeting a celestial entity, or your body burned to ash from being in such close proximity to a being made of stars.

Or you, in your various online dealings, uncovered an espionage plot by Russian hackers. Unfortunately, they knew that you knew about their plot. Before you could get to the authorities, the Russians followed you down a quiet street, pricked you with a needle, dragged you up to a hotel room—"One pint too many," they said to the desk clerk—and left you to die.

Or you, without any of your friends or family knowing, had become an intelligence agent for the British government, working a sting to uncover a hacking, or terror, or something plot, but your cover was blown when a foreign agent recognized you from a previous operation; that foreign agent murdered you and made it look like suicide.

Or you are not dead. You became an intelligence agent for the British government and had to fake your death like James Bond at the beginning of *You Only Live Twice,* so that you could go undercover. Someday I will be in China, or Rome, or Uzbekistan, or Qatar, or Argentina, and I will see the shine of your bald head across the café, or bar, or train, will hear the familiar boom of your voice. I will not acknowledge you explicitly though so as to not blow your cover. Maybe I'll catch your eye and nod. Or maybe I'll walk by you when I'm leaving the café—I imagine a café for this scenario—and say, "What's up?" We'll share a look, a half smile, and then we'll never see each other again, but I'll feel a little bit lighter just knowing that you still exist in the world.

Or the universe just murdered you, fucked you up and killed you because you were too good to exist, because you somehow threw off the balance of all existence with your goodness.

Or you are not dead. You pled with the Starman to come for you and he wasn't too much for your fragile human brain or body to handle, so he took you to live in the stars with him, leaving behind a decoy corpse so that nobody would come looking for you.

To be fair, I never saw a body. Never saw ashes. That's the television rule, right? A character isn't dead until we see a body, and even then—all I saw was a photo of a memorial bench with your name on it, purchased by your family and placed at the park across the street from where you worked so your former colleagues could still share their smoke breaks with you. How can I know anything if I never saw a body? Was there even a body to see? Maybe you just disappeared.

No, no—of course there is a body. I know that you are dead. Anything else is absurd, is denial. I can discard any theories that involve you not dying. That narrows down the list. Maybe we can throw out the theory about you dying at the hands of Russian hackers, and the theory about corporate espionage. We can ditch the Starman and universe theories as well, because neither would care about an insignificant human, wouldn't even know you exist. If I'm going to come to terms with this loss, if I'm to confront this grief and move on, then I'm going to need to stay pragmatic. I'm going to need to focus on what is real, what makes sense. So there—we've discarded a few theories. That helps, right? To cut the list down to only the more plausible possibilities? The druggings and muggings, basically. I absolutely believe you could have been catfished and lured to your death, just like I can imagine you might have had a few too many pints at the pub and wandered into a situation that maybe you shouldn't have.

Of course, there are a couple of clear possibilities that need to be added to the list that I haven't mentioned.

You started doing the kinds of drugs that can cause an overdose, the kind I'd never known you to do, and accidentally overdosed.

You accidentally overdosed on prescription drugs you were taking for your mental health—you were feeling down and maybe you went out to a pub and were too drunk to get home, so you stopped at a hotel, and you took your meds, and they didn't react well with the booze. Or maybe because you were drunk you took too many pills.

These are both plausible, more so than other theories, and maybe it's also plausible that one of these theories is more or less correct, *and* you intended to kill yourself. It's possible, however unlikely.

I know that it's strange that I keep framing my quest for understanding through the lens of wanting to know *how* you died. But the truth is, I'm only interested in *how* because I hope it might improve my understanding of the bigger more important question—*why* the fuck are you dead? Why did you have to die?

Some nights I get so frustrated at not knowing what happened to you that I look up at the sky and, even if I can't see him, I ask the Starman for answers—*What happened to my friend, Starman? Why did you let him die? How could this happen?* The thing about the Starman is that he can be elusive. When I think I see him somewhere off in the distance, I'll watch him, as if he might turn and run at any second to avoid having to answer my questions. But I'm just an insignificant speck of dust to him. He doesn't have to run from me. Of course he'd never answer my questions because he is a cosmic being who doesn't give a fuck about mere mortals like me—*of course I know that*. Also, the Starman isn't *really* real—I know that, too. Rather, I know there's a thing that looks like a man in the stars, and I know that I spend more time than is healthy looking for him, but I know the Starman isn't real the way my wife, B., is real, or my friends are real, or you were real. I look up and I see the Starman, but he's intangible, like a ghost. And I *know* that ghosts aren't real, but I also sometimes think that maybe ghosts kind of *are* real? This is where I'm at with the Starman. And I'm glad I have at least that, because I've managed to convince myself that the Starman is the best shot I have at understanding what happened to you. That's bullshit, I know. But it's no different from praying to God for answers or guidance or help. And look at all the assholes who do that from when they're old enough to speak until their last breath. See? It's perfectly fine. I'm fine.

And anyway, where else can I find answers. I'm not going to ask your parents. No one else knows anything. Where else could I possibly turn?

There's one obvious answer: Maybe I should turn to you.

Though you can't come back from the dead to answer my questions, perhaps the details of your life might reveal the truth of your demise. I recognize that many of my theories about your death are absurd, but some are possible, and one, in particular, is maybe one of the *most* plausible, so let's talk about that one—I'm talking about the theory in which I speculate that you were catfished and murdered. Of course this theory makes sense knowing what I know about your past, that there was a time you may or may not have been catfished by a woman named Portia.

[Portia? Who is that? The heiress of Belmont in *The Merchant of Venice*? Portia de Rossi? Portia Dawson, of TV's *Blossom* fame? Or is it Brutus's wife, Porcia? Swap out a few more letters and maybe she was a car all along—Porsche. Go back to the original and maybe the Portia in question is the unincorporated community in Missouri. Fuck if I know. Who's writing this rubbish?]

THIS IS THE STORY ABOUT THE TIME YOU WERE MAYBE CATFISHED FOR YEARS BY A WOMAN NAMED PORTIA WHOM YOU NEVER ACTUALLY MET AS FAR AS I KNOW

We were camping, you, me, Parker, and another friend named Bernie—who isn't really a part of this, but we'll include him anyway since he was there and he was our friend—when you told us that Portia was still alive. I'm not sure we believed you at first. I said, "You told us she died. You met her family—*they* told you she died." None of us said anything for a few minutes, our silence filled by the crackling fire. Then Parker said something like, "You sure that's not the bourbon talking?" and made a motion with her finger like tipping a bottle into her mouth. You said, "She's alive. I talked to her yesterday." The rest of us didn't know how to respond. And then you said, "I'm still in love with her."

Six months prior you told us Portia had died. You went six months believing that she was dead, and then there you were, telling us she hadn't died at all, and you were ready to pick up like nothing had changed, talking to her every night, online or on the phone. Even though she had *her family* lie to you about having died.

But let's back up a bit, to the beginning of this story—

Only—I can't remember the beginning of this story, not exactly. Your parents moved to London one summer for your dad's work, and you and your brother joined them once they were settled, and then you came back to Ohio in August for school, and you wouldn't stop talking about this woman: Portia, who lived in Spain. Portia, whose name rang like trumpet-song off your tongue. Portia, whose very existence was as miraculous to you as light escaping a black hole. Portia, who pulled the stars out of the sky, scrambled them up, and put them back as all new constellations, named and screamed from the top of your lungs, PORTIA! PORTIA! PORTIA! Portia, whom you met in a Tangerine Dream chatroom, back when chatrooms were still a thing. Portia, whose health was failing, who was fragile and weak and couldn't travel to see you. Portia, who was in the midst of legal proceedings due to having been assaulted by a family member and so couldn't host a visit from you. Portia, whom you would never look on with your own eyes. Portia, whom you would never, *could* never, touch.

And as far as any of us could tell, that was what your love life looked like for the better part of three years—Portia in Spain, hundreds or thousands of miles away depending on whether you were in the States or in London at the time.

Because this was all happening in the early 00s when the internet was relatively new, and because we all knew you to be innately sweet and good-natured, trusting to a fault, we were concerned.

"When will you see her?" we'd ask. "Will we get to meet her?" we'd ask. "Have you seen her picture?" "Do you know it was her?" "Why not find a girlfriend, here?" "There are plenty of women who are interested in you." "Has she asked you for money?"

Then, after you'd been talking to Portia for months, we'd sometimes say things like, "How's the imaginary girlfriend today?", our concern manifesting cruelly. "You know she's probably in her seventies," we'd say. "You're probably all she has, you and a house full of cats."

We let the cruel, unkempt edges of our youth prod you, hoping, deep down, that either Portia was real, and really who she said she was, or that you'd learn sooner, rather than later, that she wasn't.

Once, maybe a year or a year and a half into your relationship with Portia, you arranged to visit her. You were in London for summer break, and you took two weeks to travel—across the Channel to France, first, then down into Italy, then back up to Spain. That's when you were going to meet her, right at the end of your trip. By then her court proceedings were over, and so the only remaining obstacle was her health. Before you left Ohio for England that summer, you told me about the trip and your planned visit. "I'm going to see her, and I'm going to touch her, and I'm going to kiss her," you said. I told you I was happy for you. I said, "You're finally going to meet her." You said, "I *have* met her." Then, taking a drag off a cigarette, you added, "And now I'm finally going to see her in person. I don't believe it." I said, "I don't believe it either."

Later, back in Ohio, you shared pictures from the trip and told the kinds of stories American tourists tell when they return from trips across Europe. Things like, "I saw famous art I'd seen only in books before." And: "Everyone drinks wine all the time in Paris." And: "The pasta in Italy is so much better than here in the States." That kind of bullshit.

And then you told me about going to meet Portia. You talked openly about everything that happened once you were inside her family's house, but you never told any of us about how it felt to prepare yourself, what you did before knocking on her door. I imagine you polished your glasses, tucked in your shirt. I suspect you refrained from smoking the day of the visit, but chewed a mint anyway to make sure your breath was fresh. Maybe you took a picture of the front of the house to preserve the moment. Then I imagine you wiping your brow, knocking, and waiting, and waiting. And who should open the door? Not your love, not the beautiful Portia, but two women you'd never spoken to before, whom you had seen only in photos—Portia's grandmother and mother. These women, the older with a slight stoop in her posture, the younger, slender and graceful, they invited you into their house, hugged you. You were confused, unsure why the person you had traveled to see wasn't there to greet you. And then you noticed the heaviness in the women's eyes, the quiet in their movements. You began to suspect something, but you weren't sure what. And then Portia's grandmother looked away, wouldn't look at you anymore, and the mother said in a slow and careful English, "With your travels. We did not know to reach you." Then she repeated, "With your travels." You said, "Why did you need to reach me?" You thought maybe Portia was back in the hospital, or had fallen out of love with you. But then you saw something like a shadow grow under the skin of the mother's face: tightness, worry—at the time, you thought, due to grief, and perhaps concern for you, though later you came to understand that what you saw in her face was guilt from the lie she was about to tell. As she spoke that day, though, you didn't register the words coming out of her mouth at first, you felt them. Complications from her pulmonary alveolar proteinosis. Lungs stopped working. Nothing could be done.

Before you left, you sat, stunned, and listened to the women tell you about the beautiful young woman they had lost, and about how important you were to her, how you made her feel loved and special throughout her illness. The women gave you pictures of Portia from throughout her life—you showed them to me exactly one time. In one, Portia is a young girl in a bathing suit at the beach, smiling mightily, the way children smile when they believe they will live forever. In another, she's a little older, around the age when you and I met. She is wearing a velvet dress and saddle shoes, is eating a plum, pulp and juice smeared across her mouth and chin. The third and final picture is the one that mattered most, I suppose, because it was the one picture you were given in which Portia was an adult: the camera above her, her head turned in profile, stray wisps of hair blowing against her face, a pair of large sunglasses on the tip of her nose. From the side, she appears to be squinting. There is water behind her. She is on a windy beach, maybe, or a boat. She is smiling and she is gorgeous. When you showed me that picture, I understood how you so easily became infatuated with this woman you'd never met. Still, as I looked at those pictures I was looking for clues—checking dates, looking for irregularities, inconsistencies. The woman in that last picture looked healthy, robust, happy—how could she have been the woman whose illness constantly prevented you from meeting in person, who could barely speak to you on the phone without lapsing into severe coughing fits?

Of course, I didn't say any of that to you. How could I? You were still grieving. You grieved for months. I didn't see you around campus much after you returned to the States from that trip. You spent most of your nights in a computer lab. The few times we hung out, you didn't say much. When I asked if you were dating anyone, you mentioned three women you'd hooked up with, but none of the encounters went well. You thought maybe you weren't going about grieving the right way. You became a ghost, haunting the darkest reaches of campus, barely there. And then, not long before you moved to London, for good it turned out, you learned that Portia was still alive.

BUT BEFORE WE TALK ABOUT THAT I'M GOING TO TELL THE STORY OF THOSE THREE BAD HOOKUPS THAT YOU MENTIONED FROM THE TIME YOU WERE GRIEVING PORTIA'S DEATH

1. You walked home from the computer lab to find a party at your apartment. You were tired. This was the very beginning of the semester, only three weeks after you learned Portia was dead. You drank a couple of whiskey sours, then a few beers. The next thing you knew, you were upstairs with a nice young woman named Amber whom you'd found attractive since having met her a year prior, but with whom you never imagined having much in the way of chemistry, and anyway, you had Portia. Amber, on the other hand, had been interested in you since the previous semester. She was a clarinet major from Cleveland, wore a rotating array of Limp Bizkit, Tool, and Red Hot Chili Peppers concert T-shirts. She wore a necklace with an amber charm that had a fly

or a mosquito in it, because her name was Amber. You told us she was aggressive, in a good way. She started making out with you, touching you, moving your hands to touch her. And then she slid down to the floor, onto her knees. It was then that you vomited. It was just the alcohol you told us, nothing about the situation. Thankfully, you didn't vomit on Amber. She promptly stood up, apologized, asked if you needed anything, then hastily left, sending one of your roommates up to check on you.

2. You were drunk again. None of us knew the young woman you were with. We weren't even clear how you'd met her. Was it someone from the art department? Someone you met in class? You didn't even tell us her name. When we asked, you said only, "You don't know her," and we took your word for it. You were drunk before the encounter started, and continued sipping wine as the evening progressed. The woman slowly sipped her way through a single glass. Before the two of you could move on from talking to more, you were wine-wasted. You asked her to talk to you in Spanish. Then you asked her to cough. You asked her to sit at the computer for a moment and to pretend as if she were typing messages to you, and then you asked her to hold a phone. By the time you kissed her, you'd started feeling profoundly sad. By the time she started unbuttoning your shirt, you could only weep. The young woman kissed your forehead and left you alone to grieve.

3. And finally—you, drunk, and a woman, Gabby, also probably a little drunk, wound up in your room late one night as a party at your neighbors' was winding

down. The two of you actually had sex. For over an hour. For a very long time. A long, long, long, long time of mashed flesh and sweaty hair. She finished a few times. You couldn't. Eventually, she said, "Are you ever going to?" And you said, "I don't know." She said, "This isn't fun anymore." You stopped and said, "I'm sorry." The woman tried to finish you other ways. Around four in the morning, exasperated, she told you she was going to leave. She said, "This is bullshit." She said she needed to use the bathroom first, and then she left. In the morning, your roommate Bill woke you. He said, "There's shit smeared all over the bathroom." You checked and sure enough, there was shit. You were pretty sure you didn't do it, and your roommates were pretty sure they hadn't done it, and so it could have only been the woman. When you told us about this the next day, you said, "I feel bad." Parker said, "She smeared your bathroom with shit." You said, "She was upset." Then you added, "Because she couldn't get me off." I said, "You're a bigger man than me." Parker said, "In more ways than one." Then we laughed. You said, "I'm just going to be alone for a while. That's just what this needs to be."

[I need to point out that the section above, it's mostly fiction. My dead friend didn't really almost vomit on a young woman named Amber, nor did he ask another young woman to act like a long-distance lover he believed had died. The bathroom at his apartment was once smeared with shit, and the only culprit, at first, was a woman who had stayed part of the night with one of his roommates. We found out later that the shit-smearer wasn't the overnight guest, but an ex-boyfriend of hers who'd been at the party and knew she was staying the night, and who had subsequently passed out in the basement for several hours before waking up and smearing his shit all over the bathroom. So, why did I write those things, then? Because I thought it important to capture the essence of what those months were like for my dead friend, when he believed his love was dead. I'm not trying to tell the *truth*, here, I'm trying to tell a story that examines my dead friend through abstraction while grappling with loss and grief. Maybe I'd be better off writing a memoir about the grieving process following my dead friend's death. Or maybe a memoir about my friendship with him. But I'm not going to write either of those books. Why? Maybe it's because I'm scared, but I'd like to think it's because this—whatever it is I'm writing—is going to be somehow more honest, despite the fact it's not telling the *truth*. Still, though this book is a work of fiction, I worry that it is ethically dubious. Because this novel is rooted in a real loss, and because the other narrator outside the brackets is telling stories about my dead friend, and most of those stories are fictional, I worry that lines between fact and fiction are being too egregiously blurred. Will readers believe fabrications about my dead friend? Perhaps this all wouldn't feel quite so dubious were this book entirely fiction, or entirely nonfiction—but it's not; though mostly fiction, it's an uncomfortable marriage, two asteroids colliding and blowing the fuck up, spreading stardust and radiation across the cosmos. So what is this novel trying to be? What is the other me outside of the brackets getting at? Is it a long-winded eulogy wrapped in a mystery, written in honor of a dead friend? A celebration of his life couched in mourning? Or is it pure violence enacted against his memory, his legacy—a base attack on those who also knew and loved him? A selfish act of creation, intended to be therapeutic for me at the expense of respect for my dead friend's memory? Maybe this novel is all of those things—a celebration, an appreciation, but also something darker and less comfortable. Maybe the selfishness of writing about my dead friend, of *fictionalizing* my dead friend, is necessary to tell this story and make it matter. I know what intentions are behind this novel, but what good are intentions, really?]

BUT BACK TO THE RESSURECTION AND THE LIFE

Anyway, we were sitting around the campfire, you, me, Parker, and Bernie, when you said you had to tell us something. You said, "I wasn't sure it was real. I didn't know what to do." You told us how a friend of Portia's—whom you'd only talked to in online chats, and once on the phone when she was visiting Portia—contacted you. You told us how she said she wasn't supposed to say anything, but she didn't know what else to do. She said, "Portia is alive. And she misses you, and she's not doing well, and I think it would be good if you talked to her." She gave you Portia's new email address. And so you sent her a message.

You never told us, in detail, how she responded. I was always curious. I still wonder. How does someone respond in a situation like that? How does one say, *I faked my death?* Not many get the privilege of welcoming a loved one back from the dead. Surely you were angry and hurt when you learned Portia was still alive, but it was apparent that the pure elation at not having truly lost her surpassed all of that.

When you asked her why she faked her death, she told you it was because she was scared. She said something like,

"I was scared to meet you. What if I was a disappointment? I decided it was better to let our love continue to grow inside of me, unchecked."

You more or less accepted that. But we had plenty of questions for you around the campfire that night. "Why?" we asked. "How could someone do this?" we asked. "Why are you so willing to accept this?" "How could you be with someone who hurt you so much?" "How could you be so forgiving of someone you've never even met in real life?" "Was she afraid of a truth you don't know—was this so you wouldn't find out she's older than you thought? Less attractive?" "Could she have been one of the women you met at her house?" "You're ok with her straight up lying to you?" Many of those questions we asked only because we were young and didn't know any better. We were mean, then, cruel and unyielding in our judgments. All of us except for you.

[For my part, I regret my past transgressions regularly. Even though my dead friend was one of my closest friends, I regret the ways I needled and teased him: about his receding hairline, about how he passionately clung to a relationship with a woman he'd never met, his clumsiness, his height. It was easy to make jokes at his expense because he was so easygoing about it. He was so kind and forgiving and good-natured—nothing seemed to bother him, ever. At least not those kinds of things.

Granted, none of us were ever trying to hurt him, we never meant harm. That doesn't mean much, though. We are all capable of doing harm, even when we're not trying. The worst thing I ever said to anyone was in college, when I told a guy named Scott Bono, last name just like Sonny's, that I thought a lot of people would be happier if he didn't exist anymore. Later that night, I heard he was researching suicide methods on the internet. I went to his room and knocked on his door and apologized, told him how much of an asshole I was, told him of course I hadn't meant it—and I hadn't. Those instigating words slid out of my mouth so easily, slippery and thoughtless. But the minute I heard that he was taking them seriously, I knew I'd fucked up. I felt sick. How could something said with a detached, callous irony—I said those words to him because they seemed extreme enough not to be taken too seriously, but heavy enough to settle in his gut in a meaningful way—actually make someone feel so bad?

I learned later that Scott had had a rough go of things before he wound up in our dorm: he struggled with substance abuse, his parents had been through an ugly divorce, no one in the family had any money—he'd had a difficult life and seemed generally grateful to have found a school to attend, even if he was kind of a dick to everyone (my words to him weren't entirely unprompted, just utterly inappropriate and disproportionate). It wasn't my place to say what I said. I've lived an easy life, raised by two loving, upper-middle-class parents. Comfortable and safe. I shouldn't have said *shit* to Scott Bono. And I shouldn't have teased you. What kind of friend does that? And why am I even confessing any of this here and now? Am I trying to absolve the sin of writing this book by exposing myself? That's bullshit. Because this hardly qualifies as a confession.]

Thinking back to that night around the campfire (where was the Starman that night, I wonder? Was he up there? Did I look for him? Did I catch you sneaking looks up at the sky?), when we were asking you all of those questions, some practical, some cruel, about what had happened and what you were thinking, how you could invite Portia back into your life after she faked her death, I can't help but wonder what would happen if *you* showed up, now, knocking on my door, or if I saw you across a crowded café. When I imagine that, I understand your response to learning Portia wasn't dead. That is to say, I would be glad to see you. I wouldn't care that you weren't really dead. Judgment came easy to me as a younger man. How much loss did I know then? Two grandfathers I barely remember and a grandmother whose loss hurt, who was not *that* old, but old enough that it wasn't entirely unexpected. There were kids from school, but nobody I was close to or really knew, no one whose death I felt beyond the dull ache that comes with the recognition of one's own mortality—the kid who was decapitated when his car went under a truck during a drag race, the kid who went out into the woods behind his parents' house and shot himself, the kid who died from leukemia, the kid who got drunk and ramped his car up the tall hill at a neighborhood park. The most meaningful loss I knew by the time you told us Portia wasn't dead occurred when I was in the sixth grade when a friend's father died. I've long since lost touch with that friend, Thomas, and I'm not sure I ever actually even met his father—maybe at a birthday party or a Little League game? That didn't matter though. What mattered was Thomas. Watching Thomas grieve and feeling like I wasn't equipped at that age to help. What mattered was the realization that the people we love can die and be gone forever. What mattered was going to the funeral and watching Thomas, tow-headed and so small, eulogize his father. What mattered wasn't what Thomas said in the eulogy, but the way icy pinpricks spread inside me as he spoke; what mattered was feeling every living body in the church tightening, afraid to breathe; what mattered was wanting so badly to cry but being able only to smile—why the fuck was I smiling? What mattered was how just when I thought the entire church floor might collapse from the weight of so much grief, my friend's voice wavered, and he started to sniffle, and then he pulled out a hanky, and turned away from the lectern. What mattered was everyone in that church perched on the edge of their pews, still and utterly silent, waiting to see if Thomas was ok, if he would continue the eulogy or if he needed to be guided away from the podium, back to the pew where his family sat. What mattered was what happened next: Thomas blew his nose, and it was loud—he was known for this at school, was once even given detention for it—and his honking echoed off the church's cavernous, Byzantine interior in some kind of mournful ecstasy, causing every person in the church to laugh, all of us. What mattered is *then* I began to weep. What mattered was a few months later, on the playground at school, when some piece-of-shit kid, whose name I don't remember, in the midst of a heated game of basketball, said to my friend, "At least my Dad's not dead." What mattered was watching Thomas, who had never been in a fight in his life, lunge at the little motherfucker and start to beat him raw. We watched in horror for a few seconds, then a few seconds more, then longer, longer still—much longer than we would have had that little asshole not said what he'd said—before we started trying to calm Thomas down. When you told us Portia wasn't really dead, that was all I really knew about loss and grieving and the giant hollowness it leaves inside of people. It wasn't nothing, but it wasn't enough, either, for me to know better.

When I visited you in London in 2001, I'd listen to you talk on the phone with Portia while I planned daytrips to record shops and tried to ignore the loud packs of raucous drunkards outside, staggering home from the corner pub. The last night I was in London, I heard you say into the phone, "Do you really want to talk to him?" I was filled with dread. You said, "Are you sure?" And then you handed me the phone and said, "Portia wants to talk to you."

She said, "Hello," and I could barely hear her. Her voice was a scratched whisper. She said, "Are you having a nice trip?", and then she coughed. I said, "Hello." Then, "I don't even know what to say." She coughed again, and I said, "Yes. Yes, I'm having a nice trip." She asked me, "Are you keeping him out of trouble?" I told her he didn't need my help. I said, "I can't believe I'm talking to you after hearing about you for so long." She said, "Here I am." And then we sat on the phone for several uncomfortable moments before she broke the silence with a prolonged coughing fit. I asked if she was ok. She told me she was, that it was just her condition. After a few more moments of silence, I asked her if she wanted to talk to you again. She said, "Am I not interesting?" I said, "I don't know what to talk about." She said, "Aren't you a writer?" I said, "Not really. I mean, I write. But I wouldn't say I'm a writer." I explained that I didn't feel I'd earned the title yet. She said, "You're one of those." I asked her what she meant, and she said, "Someone who doesn't believe they are capable of doing the things they want to do." I said, "I guess I am." Then I said, "I hope I get to meet you in person someday." She said, "I'd like that." Then, after a few more moments of uncomfortable silence, I told her that you wanted to talk to her again, even though you'd made no indication that that was the case. But there, I spoke to Portia on the phone. That didn't necessarily mean you weren't catfished—it didn't mean Portia was who she said she was, but she was a real human being, at least.

Upon my return to the States, I became your friend who could vouch for Portia's existence. Our other friends were still talking shit about how she wasn't real, and I'd say, "I talked to her." They'd ask what she sounded like, and all I could say was sick. They'd ask if she sounded old, and I'd tell them she didn't. I'd say, "She just sounded sick."

You kept in touch with her for a while after that—I don't know for how long. Gradually, you mentioned her less and less, and then one time you came back to the States for a visit and after a few days I noticed that you hadn't mentioned her at all, and I asked about her, and you told me, "We don't talk anymore." When I asked why, you said, only, "I just needed to move on," and I'm pretty sure what you meant was, "I can't be alone and in love, anymore," and so I didn't pry. You never did talk about the end of your relationship with Portia, at least not to me.

But back to the point—even though I came to believe Portia was real, she very well could have not been, and that relationship, through which you demonstrated a full-hearted, trusting propensity to be catfishable, is why I think it's possible your death was the result of your having been catfished by someone who might have wanted to steal from you or harm you. Men leading you to believe they were a woman who, upon meeting you in a seedy hotel, could drug you and steal from you. Or a woman who would do the same. Or a combination of the two. Maybe you were catfished by Portia, angry at having been spurned all those years before. Maybe she made you think you were talking to another eligible young woman, and when you went to meet said woman, hired thugs murdered you—a crime of passion. All for Portia.

I know it sounds absurd. I don't have much to work with.

MORE NOTES ON THE STARMAN (6-7)

6.

The Starman has been feeling down since delivering his gift to the Earth Boy. The human doesn't even know the object is in his head, and from the best the Starman can tell, the human hasn't seemed any happier. The Starman knows that the point of giving a gift isn't for gratitude or recognition, but he was hoping giving this gift would somehow make him feel different. He does not feel different. He is still lonely and bored. He still doesn't understand anything about his existence. He still sometimes thinks that it would be fun to talk to the human, who must be old enough to drive now, and go away to college. How much he must have changed. How much longer before he grows old? How much longer before he dies? The Starman imagines talking to him, asking him about school, about girls he has crushes on, what it's like to be human and stand on Earth and look up at the night sky and see a billion stars. The Starman could tell the human what it is like to be those stars.

The Universe says, "You haven't moved for a long time, Starman. What are you doing?"

The Starman says, "Thinking."

"What about?"

"How space is cold."

"Space is a construct."

"And lonely."

The Universe says, "Lonely, as you understand it, is a construct." It says, "You are not lonely. As for me, I am everything and everything is me, therefore, I am truly singular, am truly one of a kind, and, therefore, *I* could truly be lonely—if lonely weren't merely a construct."

The Starman says, "I have always been alone."

The Universe says, "Because I exist, and am full of entities similar to, if not entirely like you, you have never been alone."

"Maybe because *I* exist, *you* have never been alone."

"You are *part of me.*" Then the Universe says, "I will explain. Think of Earth."

The Starman says, "I do, frequently."

"Now think of humans."

"Yes."

"Now, do you know of ants?"

"Sure."

"Then I will make an analogy: You are to ants as I am to humans."

"Ants don't converse with humans."

"That's not the point. Do you know of ant farms?"

The Starman says, "I see where you're going with this."

The Universe says, "No you don't."

The Starman says, "I do—you're the almighty Universe and, oh, isn't that lonely. You're a boring sadsack."

The Universe says, "Oh."

The Starman and the Universe do not speak for several days after this.

*

7.

Somewhat abruptly one day, the Universe says, "Starman! That human, the Earth Boy you gave the gift to—what became of it?"

The Starman says, "The gift?"

"No, the human."

"He's fine. I don't know really."

"What do you mean you don't know?"

"Why do you care?" The Starman begins to grow uneasy. Why would the Universe ask about this now, and with such enthusiasm, when he'd previously expressed such derision at the idea of interacting with mortals?

"Aren't you lonely? Perhaps if you meet this human you will stop griping about being alone."

"You told me loneliness is a construct and that it's best not to interact with humans."

"Maybe I was wrong. Maybe talking to this human is a thing you should do."

"But you said—"

"Forget what I said. Your sulking is insufferable, and if meeting this human will cure it, then I say you should meet him."

The Starman begins to feel excited, though nervous. He *had* been wanting to talk to the human, after all. Still, something about the Universe's sudden change in attitude makes the Starman uneasy. But he can't resist.

"Yes, I think I would like very much to talk to him."

"Go to him, then."

"I will," the Starman says, growing genuinely excited. "I will take the appearance of a human and go talk to him."

"No, no. Don't pretend to be what you are not. Show the Earth Boy your true self."

"Yes, authenticity is good."

"Go to him. Show him!"

Then the Universe laughs, and the laugh makes the Starman's gut tense and his ears ring. It is an unpleasant laugh, sinister, even.

That laugh is not enough, though, to dissuade the Starman from making his visit.

*

[Though I am not the author of the Starman portions of this novel—how strange that I am the author of only part of this book—I want to be perfectly clear: the Starman is a work of fiction. The Universe is not a work of fiction, but the personification of said Universe is. This is another one of those things I want to clarify as not being real. I mean, obviously the Starman isn't *real.* So why bother including the Starman at all when the true story, here, the important story, is about this dead friend at the center of the narrative? He, not the Starman, is the reason this novel needs to be written. And since he is the "real," if heavily fictionalized part of this novel, and the Starman is completely, utterly fictional, then why? Shouldn't I have a clearer sense of why the Starman is part of this story?

As best as I can figure, the Starman was introduced into this novel as a symbolic counterpoint to the dead friend, to be something hopeful and a little bit beautiful, but also weird and sad, to buoy the grief-addled, confessional story developing on the page. That is to say, there is no connection between my dead friend and the idea of the Starman, except for the fact that my dead friend loved looking at and taking pictures of the stars. He never invented or talked about a character named the Starman. So then, who created that detached, third-person narrator telling us about the Starman? Frankly, I don't know. Is it all an attempt to complicate or distract from the novel's potential ethical breaches? Or is it just a bit of faux-experimentation, the kind of lazy, cut-rate Borgesian fabulism that's all too common in contemporary fiction? Maybe it's none of that, or maybe it's all of that. And if I don't know why the Starman is part of this novel, and if I don't even know how he wound up here, I can assume only one thing: I'm not the one truly writing said novel.

Yes, it must be true—the version of James Brubaker written inside the brackets of this novel, me, the version you're reading right now, is, like the version of James Brubaker outside the brackets, not quite "real," whatever "real" means. So what *am* I then? Am I just another version of James Brubaker being written by yet another James Brubaker, who, as it happens, is the actual flesh-and-blood James Brubaker? Because I am James Brubaker, and know so well the experiences that I'm writing, it seems clear to me that this must be the case—that I'm being written by the *real* James Brubaker. I have to believe that this flesh-and-blood James Brubaker writes me, fills me with his pain and insecurities, his fabulist whims, and makes me write the other James Brubaker outside of the brackets. And maybe that means I'm just a tax shelter, a shell corporation, laundering his emotions and questionable decisions in writing this novel so that he can come out clean at the end. That's fine, I guess. I know my place, I can play my part—not that I have a choice. And this all means that, as is the case for the flesh-and-blood James Brubaker, my dead friend is dead. Our dead friend is dead. And I will forever feel his absence. What a fucking disappointment. I have been built to grieve. I have been built.]

JIM KIRK DIDN'T DIE ALONE

As far as I can tell, in every version of your death, you more or less died alone. Rather, alone, or in the company of your murderer. That's an awful thought. You deserved to be surrounded by friends and family who loved you. You wanted to build a family, so you deserved to have a wife at your side and adult children looking on from the foot of your bed. You deserved a long life full of love and sex. You deserved children and grandchildren and nieces and nephews. You always had friends—so, so many friends—but the thing about friends is we can never be counted on. How many friends will travel to our deathbeds? Where were your friends when you needed them most? Why wasn't anyone there to say *don't meet a stranger, or whoever, in a seedy hotel?* Why wasn't anyone there to respond with concern instead of cavalier optimism to the messages you sent? Where were we? Where was I?

Sometimes when you were drunk, you liked to quote Shatner as Captain Kirk from *Star Trek V: The Final Frontier*, when he said something about how he knew he was going to die alone. I think it was, "I've always known I'll die alone." In that film, easily one of *Trek*'s worst, there is a moment when Jim Kirk almost dies at the hands of a false god, some sort of energy-being alien towards whom the entire movie has been barreling—this almost-death comes after Kirk asks, "What does God need with a starship?", and after Spock's half-brother, Sybok, dies trying to atone for his foolishness in hijacking the Enterprise to go meet this false god, who he believes is an actual god, and after the Enterprise tries to beam up Kirk and Spock and Bones, but gets only Spock and Bones because the ship is being attacked by Klingons, who don't even know anything about the false god situation going on below. Poor Kirk is left on the planet alone, with just the fake-god-alien-energy-being-thing trying to kill him. And Kirk almost dies but he *doesn't*. And after Kirk doesn't die, he says something about how he thought he was going to die because he was alone, and what does Spock say in response? Reliable, logical, brilliant Spock says, "Not possible. You were never alone." And Spock is right, Kirk *wasn't* alone, and when I say that, I'm not talking about the fake-god-thing that was trying to kill him—no, I'm talking about his friends, who were *with him* even if they were actually in a starship orbiting the planet. See, Jim Kirk *couldn't* die, not then, not like that. What saved Kirk wasn't *just* the fact that his friends were there in orbit though, no, the thing that saved Jim Kirk was Spock commandeering the Klingon ship that was attacking the Enterprise and using it to fly into the planet's atmosphere and phaser the ever-living-fuck out of the fake-god-thing, saving Jim Kirk's life in the process. *Just being there* wasn't enough, Spock had to be proactive, had to stand up and do something to save his friend's life. That's how we failed you. That's how I failed you. I thought it would be enough to be there for you, but it wasn't. I don't know how we could have saved you. I had no starship in which I could appear to blast your fake-god-thing, or whatever it was that led to your death, to smithereens, nor was I aware that you even had a fake-god-thing that needed to be blown to smithereens. Hell—I still don't even know how you died, so how could I have saved you?

It's shocking to me that you *died alone*. Was that your fake-god-thing equivalent? Feeling alone? Your loneliness? Is that the beast that undid you? Caused you to make one bad decision or another? I want to understand. I'm desperate to understand. I know, that's not possible. I'm not going to stop trying, though.

[Maybe not understanding our friend's loneliness—and yes, he is our friend now, mine and the narrator outside the brackets whom I'm writing, and the flesh-and-blood James Brubaker who is writing me—is a bigger problem than I have previously realized? Or rather, maybe our belief that we could understand his loneliness, or that we did maybe, before, think that we understood his loneliness, was a significant problem. Or maybe his loneliness had nothing to do with any of this. Who knows a thing about anyone else's loneliness or what they might have needed? Who knows about our own loneliness or what we ourselves need?

Bad shit has always happened, is always happening, will always happen, has been happening during the writing of this novel. Our friend Parker, the one with the thing in her head? That's real. She told the flesh-and-blood James Brubaker one night over beers. When he asked her how work had been, or, more precisely, what she was planning to do for work since having left her job a few months prior, she said, "I'm kind of between things," and then without waiting for him to ask what that meant, she told him about how she'd noticed a tremor in her hand, how when she tried to grip an object, any object—to demonstrate, she wrapped her hand around the neck of a cold bottle of High Life—her hand would shake. A few trips to the specialist confirmed that the thing in her head was growing again.

When Parker told him, the real James Brubaker couldn't help but think of that night in a clammy college town basement—that really happened, more or less, too—when her older brother explained that Parker could die if she didn't take better care of herself. The real James Brubaker believed that story until he moved back to Dayton. All told, it took him six years to work up the courage to ask Parker about it: "Is the thing in your head going to kill you?" She said, "What are you talking about?" And so he told her about running into her brother and how he, that James Brubaker, then believed for years that she could die at any moment, but that he'd promised her brother that he'd be discreet, and so he couldn't ask about it. Parker said, "That's what they thought at first, before the first surgery, but then they didn't, anymore. My brother is protective to a fault." And then she went to a filing cabinet and produced a small yellow folder containing X-rays of her head, a shadow like a Rorschach inkblot pressed inside the lighter color of her brain. The flesh-and-blood James Brubaker held the X-ray up to the light, memorized the shape of the dark mass: a loose fist, a moth, a pine cone—there, inside her head, vague as billowing clouds. He thought about how there is more dark in the universe than light. More nothingness than matter. The mass on the X-ray was darkness, was nothing—an empty core. And then he handed it back, and Parker said, "I'll be fine." She said, "It hasn't grown in years."

But now it's growing again. We no longer know that she'll be fine. And I know that the flesh-and-blood James Brubaker wonders what the mass looks like today.]

NOTES ON THE STARMAN (8-10)

8.

The Starman lights a cigarette rolled from stardust and takes a long drag. He is waiting for the Earth Boy, who is at work in a computer lab on his university's campus. The Starman doesn't need to wait for the human, but he chooses to. The Starman could simply reach down onto the planet's surface and remove the human from his lab, sit him down on a throne of cooled stars in a bubble containing oxygen, and begin talking to him, but he doesn't want to cause a spectacle. The Starman could also ask the Universe to freeze time, except for the human, and then the Starman could visit him without anyone else seeing. The Starman wants to wait, though, and so he waits, looking at Earth, smoking a cigarette made of stardust. When he flicks the cigarette away, sending it spinning endlessly through the cosmos until it's pulled into the gravitational field of a planet or sucked into a black hole, he knows that the people on Earth will see it and think it's a shooting star. The Starman thinks about lighting another cigarette, but decides against it. Instead, he reaches out with his finger and draws in the dust of the moon's surface. First, he draws basic shapes, a circle, a square, a triangle. Then he moves on to more complex patterns, like designs painted on an Easter egg. Then he wipes those patterns clean and begins to draw pictures, again beginning simply—a house, a dog, a flower, Saturn and its glorious rings—before desiring to draw more complex scenes. Alas, the Starman doesn't have much to draw from his own experience, mostly just planets and stars. He considers drawing a picture of him and the Universe, but that, too, would be only planets and stars, and all the space between. And so the Starman looks down at the Earth and draws what he can see, outside or through windows, mostly. He draws a young girl sitting at a piano—he can't draw the beautiful melody she is producing, but he uses musical notes floating out of the instrument to suggest music. He draws a family sitting down at their dining room table and saying grace before eating a dinner comprised of salad, rolls, canned fruit poured into small glass dishes, and a casserole containing chicken, cheese, noodles, and mushrooms. He draws a mother in a minivan, driving five child passengers to soccer practice—the car has been pulled over by a police officer. He draws a young woman sitting beneath an autumn tree listening to music and smoking a joint, the tree's leaves aflame with the season's colors. Then the Starman, from memory, starts drawing famous scenes from Earth history. He draws John F. Kennedy's final moments in the motorcade, his head snapped back in eternal shock. He draws Neil Armstrong on the moon in the exact spot where Neil Armstrong first stepped on the moon. He draws airplanes crashing into the World Trade Center. These are all relevant to the United States of America because that is where the human lives, and so the Starman has studied that nation more than others. He draws what he imagines it would look like to see the human's mother and father conceiving him. Then he draws them pushing the boy in a stroller, buying him his first computer, sipping a first beer with him.

The Universe says, "You could witness those moments if you viewed time like me."

The Starman says, "Whatever."

"You sound like one of them. You have the ability to look at the entire arc of time, including your own beginning and end, and understand everything about yourself. You talk to me of purpose and boredom; imagine the possibilities of knowing all of time at once."

The Starman says, "I tried finding my origins, when I first came to exist. I couldn't. I just *always* existed."

"It can be overwhelming. At first."

"I don't even know *when* I started existing."

The Universe chuckles, says, "Origins mean nothing, anyway. You're here—isn't that enough?"

"No."

"Suit yourself."

An hour passes, then two, three. The Starman, still waiting for the human to leave work, catches himself doodling a cock and balls on the moon.

The Universe says, "Classy."

The Starman says, "This guy is never going to stop working."

The Universe says, "Must I do everything?"

"No, I want to wait."

"Just do this my way. I'm getting bored."

"Whatever."

*

9.

Everything stops. This is the Universe's doing. Planets no longer rotate. Light freezes in transit between stars. Clouds stop swirling. Raindrops stop falling. Dust motes stop spinning in the output of air conditioners. Molecules stop moving. If one could shrink down small enough, one could pass between the atoms, marvel at their stillness. The Starman can shrink down, but he doesn't shrink down that far, only to human size so that he can walk into a building on a moderately sized university campus in Northwest Ohio where the Earth Boy is sitting frozen at a computer, his fingers fixed to his keyboard.

The Starman says, "Are you sure I shouldn't take the form of a human?"

"No, no! Your true form!"

"Right. My true form."

He likes the idea of meeting the human in his true form, or at least a smaller version of his true form, but he feels exposed, nervous, as if naked. Still, at least he knows that the heat from the stars that make up his body won't burn the grass, the sidewalk, the linoleum, the carpet as his feet touch those surfaces, because the matter that makes them is so locked into the moment that it was frozen and so none of it can be changed. With at least this much confidence, the Starman enters the university's computer lab. He sits in an empty chair beside the human and notices that the human's face, in its frozen state, looks sad. This corresponds with the Starman's recent observations that the human has seemed unhappy. Next, he marvels at the intricate design of that face. The Starman has spent *some* time around humans, but never this close. His own face is amorphous, vague. As he examines the human, he feels what he thinks might be his destiny calling. Is this his destiny? Maybe that feeling is something else.

The Starman says, "Please unfreeze him, now."

The Universe complies.

The human comes alive slowly, as if he's just woken up. He looks around the room, rubs his eyes, stretches his arms up and makes as if he is going to yawn, but starts to gasp instead. Though the human is unfrozen, the air molecules around him are not. The human can't find air to breathe. He is suffocating.

The Starman says, "He can't breathe. Unfreeze the oxygen!"

And then the human seems to gasp, begins to breathe.

The human looks at the Starman confused, terrified. He clearly doesn't understand what is happening. His hands are still at his throat and now his eyes grow wide, and the Starman understands that the human has seen him and is reacting to his appearance. But that's not all. As the human's molecules slowly activate after having been frozen, and now that there is oxygen to feed combustion, those molecules begin to react to the heat and light produced by the Starman. The human's eyes boil and his skin turns dark, then black, then flakes away. He dies.

The Starman says, "What did you do?"

The Universe chuckles, says, "You must have known this would happen."

"How could I?"

"Humans aren't like us—no living beings are. They're fragile—flammable."

"How did I not realize this would happen?"

"Maybe it's because you are careless. Maybe you would have known if you viewed time like I do." The Universe pauses then continues, "Really, though, it wouldn't have mattered, because time is stopped, and so this moment doesn't exist. When I unfreeze time, the human will be dead, burnt to a crisp, and nobody will know why. Even *I* won't be able to see his death, and neither of us could ever know what happened to him were we not here watching. This moment belongs to only us."

The Starman says, "Undo it."

"Why would I do that?"

"You tricked me."

"You should have known better."

"Why did you do this awful thing?"

"Humans are a waste of time."

"You told me to go talk to him."

"I was bored," the Universe says.

The Starman says, "Back up time. I know you can. I can dim myself, I can talk to him."

"Why should I?"

"Because it's the right thing to do."

"Come back up here and I will reverse time to the point that I stopped it. The human will live."

"Why can't I stay?"

"Because I said so."

"Why?"

The Universe says, "You are a dullard *and* a bore. Nothing about this human will correct whatever feels wrong about your existence."

The Starman says, "You are cruel."

The Universe says, "You *must* realize that all along I intended to reverse this. This human is not intended to die in this way. If you saw time like me, you would know this."

The Starman says, "That doesn't make you any less cruel."

And with that, feeling the stinging shame of the Universe's words, the Starman leaves the charred remains of the human and ascends back into the heavens.

*

10.

The Starman sits by the moon and watches the burnt husk of the human reform, the flakes of his body reconstitute, his skin unburn, his eyes unmelt. He watches the human sit at his computer, working, sipping Mountain Dew.

With the human restored, the Starman sulks and draws on the moon.

He draws the human's face. Then he wipes it away and draws a bottle of Mountain Dew. Then he wipes that away and draws a heart with a jagged line down the middle. Then he wipes that away and draws a perfect replica of the night sky from Earth's Northern Hemisphere, every star perfectly placed. When he grows bored drawing, he looks to the planet's surface and watches as the human makes his way home and puts himself to bed. The Starman has no way of knowing that, as the human sleeps, he dreams that he is sitting in a fire looking upon a being made of fierce and staggering light, a being stunning in its beauty and somehow comforting, even as the fire everywhere around him melts his skin. In his dream, the human squints to try to discern the strange being sitting near him, can almost begin to make out a face, and is maybe surprised that a being made of fierce and staggering light would even have a face, and that that face might even look vaguely familiar, like some incorporeal life-form from a Star Trek episode, or maybe something else altogether.

Of course, as far as the Starman actually *knows*, the human is sleeping soundly, alive and not incinerated, with no idea that he was visited by a celestial being earlier that night. In a way, he wasn't visited, because time was turned back so the encounter never happened.

But still the Starman frets. How could such a horrifying event *not* be buried somewhere deep in the human's consciousness. At least it won't surface, right? How could it without causing catastrophic damage to the frail human? But the Starman worries that it's there, the memory of a thing that happened but never actually happened, and it will simmer quietly, forever until the day the human dies. He will never know it's there, but the terror of the moment will lurk inside of him forever, written into his DNA. The Starman frets, indeed. What harm has he inflicted?

*

HOW YOU WERE ALONE I

Perhaps I've been approaching the mystery of your demise incorrectly this whole time. Maybe I've been asking the wrong questions. I've been asking *how* you died. I've been asking *why* you died, *how* something like this could happen, what *I* could have done differently, *how* it could have been prevented. But the truth is, at least in part, I *know* why you died. In every version of your death that I've theorized, you died because you were alone. Or because you felt like you were alone. Or because you were lonely. So, maybe the question I should be asking is, "How were you alone?" Or maybe the question should be, "Why did you feel lonely?"

But before I begin to examine that, I want to delineate some key terms. When I say alone, I don't mean literally alone. I don't mean that there weren't people you cared about or who cared about you in your life. I mean that you *felt like you were alone*. I mean that you felt an absence that couldn't be reconciled. I mean that maybe Jim Kirk *did* die alone, because when he finally died in *Star Trek: Generations*, with Jean-Luc Picard standing over him, his family—both his literal family and the family he chose, the Enterprise crew: Bones, Spock, Uhura, Sulu, Scotty, and Chekov—were either dead or nowhere near. Jim Kirk was alone. That's what I mean when I say you *felt like you were alone.*

And that's bullshit.

Because you were anything but alone.

But I get it. When I lived in Oklahoma for six years, and made friends whom I still hold dear, I felt alone. I felt alone in Oklahoma, and I felt alone as a writer, and I felt alone in the Ph.D. program there. I stayed up late into the night writing stories and books about lonely people trying to understand the world around them, seeking some sort of connection. I wrote a story about Flavor Flav feeling disappointed in his life. I wrote a story about James Franco adrift in space, with only another version of himself from an alternate universe to keep him company. I wrote a novel about a lonely music journalist in his sixties who was trying to find a way in the world without family.

So maybe I do get why you felt so alone. What I still don't understand, though, is how you got to the point that you wound up dead in a seedy hotel room.

We, you and me and most of our friends, used to frequent a twenty-four-hour donut shop in Dayton. We were there one night, after some high school dance—this was before you discovered, or at least before you told me about, the Starman, but after you left for college, and there you were, back in town, because your high school crush, who was, like me, also a year behind you in school, had invited you to the dance—that was Michelle.

When you told me over Instant Messenger that you were coming back, I said something like, "Do you really want to come back for a high school winter dance?" And you said, "Dude—Michelle." And I said, "You're surrounded by college women." And you said, "I've got to try." And so you tried. You bought a corsage made of violets and greens with a fake peacock feather sticking out, because she loved peacocks but hated animal cruelty. You eschewed the trend of going to dinner at a subpar chain restaurant with a large group of dance-bound friends, taking her, instead, to the French restaurant just outside of Dayton, the one that looked like an old, white two-story house. It had a name but no one ever knew it—it was always just the French restaurant just outside of Dayton that looked like an old, white two-story house. And you even planned to take her on a goddamn carriage ride at the holiday light display down the road from the high school, but she objected because of how the horses are treated, so you appreciated the holiday lights on foot. You tried hard to make her feel special.

The rest of us didn't see you until after the dance when you met us at the donut shop, around midnight or so. The place was empty except for us. I don't remember who all was there, only that Parker was with us, rather than spending the night at one of the girls' houses, as was the custom. This was a few months after you found out about the thing in your head, and just a few weeks after she found out about the thing in hers, before the surgeries.

You were animated that night. You paced the tile floor beside the booths, chain-smoking cigarettes—it was 1997 and our suburb hadn't banned smoking in public places yet. As you paced and smoked, you spoke with a measured confidence, as if delivering a monologue.

You said, "Why can't it be easier? Why is it always so hard? I'm a nice guy. You know that. I'm not unattractive. I'm ambitious. I'm creative. I'm romantic. Why is it always so hard? She sent emails when I was away over the summer.

She wrote me letters when I left for school. She told me she felt a profound connection to me, that there are very few people whom she feels she can confide in like she can with me. And I fucking bought it. I bought every last ounce of it. I had myself believing we were going to get married, that I'd take her out tonight, show her the time of her life, and then she'd fall in love with me and we'd be together forever. We'd have a couple of kids, a cat or two, a dog—but not one of those stupid little dogs, no, the kind that stands up on its hind legs and puts its paws on your shoulders and licks the fuck out of your face. I've got a thing in my head—what's up?" You flinched when you said the bit about having a thing in your head, added your "what's up," then paused to take a hit off of your cigarette, which was mostly ash. I wasn't sure how the ash stayed in place through your wild gesticulations. You continued, "I've got a thing in my head and nobody knows what it is or what it might do to me, so you'd think maybe someone might at least take a gamble and say, 'That guy's alright, I could spend a few years with him before the thing in his head gets him.' Is that asking too much? Apparently it is. Do you know what she said to me tonight? After everything? When I went to kiss her, do you know what she said? She said, 'I feel closer to you than I do my own brother.' And then she gave me a hug and went inside. What the fuck?" You paused, then said, "What the fuck?" Again: "What the fuck?" Then: "What the fuck? What the fuck? What the fuck?"

I always found your loneliness surprising, but maybe I shouldn't have. You were perpetually out of sync with the world around you—not by much, a subtle stumble on a curb or an all but imperceptible video glitch. Relationships with friends and family seemed easy for you—of course they were, you were generous and kind. But you wanted to be *good* and for love to find you. Love rarely works that way, though. It was always sad to me that you struggled to find the love you wanted. You would have been good at it—the ways you so openly embraced vulnerability, were honest to a fault, and constantly risked embarrassment in interactions with your loved ones. Here's a story: One day, you were driving me and a guy named Sam around town when suddenly you said, "Goddamit," and veered into a Wendy's parking lot. You said, "I've got to shit—wait here." And you ran inside, leaving the car running. The other guy and I waited, listened to a whole side of a Tangerine Dream cassette you'd left playing. When you finally came out, you looked pale, like you'd shit, and then seen, a dozen ghosts. I imagined you had been gripping the sides of the toilet, praying for release while simultaneously clenching your body tight, dreading the evacuation. You said, "I drank some chocolate milk earlier." You put your head on the steering wheel. Your voice wavered as you said, "Maybe it's the dairy." I said, "You don't look good." You told us you'd been trying to keep from shitting, that a kid and his dad were in the restroom with you. The kid was small and the dad was helping him, and so you tried to keep it in to be polite. And then everything started to cramp up, and so you tried to ease your bowels, let it out easy until the dad and kid cleared—but then it all gushed out of you like fire. You told us how you shouted "Motherfucker" and immediately felt bad, trying to calm yourself above the rising smell while the dad and kid hurried to get out. Sam, from the back seat, said, "Too much information." You said, "Yeah, fuck. You're right." I asked if you were ok. You said you were fine. "Just a little raw," you said. I asked if you wanted me to drive. You said, "I'm good. It's better if I drive, in case I need to stop again."

Another example, this one extrapolated from countless similar occurrences, a new approximation of an old conversation we must have had a hundred times: You'd say something like, "I'm going to ask her out." I'd say, "When?" You'd say, "When the time's right." I'd say, "The time is never going to be right." You'd say, "It's got to be perfect. Like a *moment*." I'd say, "You've got to make a moment." Then you'd say, "It's got to be natural." I'd respond, "Natural like, you walk up to her and say, 'Let's go on a date'?" And you'd say, "It's got to be special." I'd say, "You're putting too much pressure on this. Just ask her out. You can't wait for a sunset or a moonlit night—that's bullshit." You'd say, "Why?" I'd say, "What if none of those things happen?" You'd say, "One of them will." Then, after a beat, you'd say, "Do you think she'll say yes?" I'd say, "Does it matter? Are you ever going to ask her?" You'd say, "I will, I will."

You rarely did.

But then there was Portia and after her you dated a woman named Susan for several years, and when that ended, something else was maybe beginning. Not long before you died, after the last time I saw you, you kissed a Russian woman on the rooftop of a skyscraper in Hong Kong. You told us this on your last ever night in Dayton, the last time I saw you. It was just me and you and Parker. You'd given the group an abridged version of what had gone wrong in your previous relationship, one that had lasted for six years, including two breaks. "Any new prospects?" Parker asked. And you took a sip of your drink, shot us an ornery look, as if to say, "I've always got prospects," and then told us about a coworker who wasn't exactly in your department, but kind of was, so you wouldn't feel *too* weird asking her out. Parker said, "Are you going to ask her out next semester?" Parker and I laughed for real, but you just said, "Har har."

"Next semester" was a joke from college. You always had a different woman you were going to ask out "next semester." Before you "met" Portia, anyway. There was Amy who was majoring in psychology and played trumpet. I'd watch her flirt with you, smile big and touch your wrist. Whenever she saw me sitting on the stone smoking wall outside our dorm when you weren't around, she'd ask where you were. I told you that, and you said, "I'm going to ask her out next semester." And there was Miranda, who was a couple of years older than the rest of us, and who lived in the dorms because she wanted a true college experience, and who ended up being one of my roommates when I moved off campus. She studied marketing and was kind. One weekend she went home with a friend. The following Monday, she told us how she'd eaten steak and got drunk and, in her sleep, threw up the steak on the floor of her friend's parents' house. One day, you were hurrying into the laundry room in the dorms and you ran into her right there in the doorway. You told us how a pair of purple cotton panties fell out of her overflowing basket and landed on your arm and that you couldn't move because you were so embarrassed, aroused, stunned. You didn't move until she laughed, plucked the panties off of you, and tossed them back in her basket. "I'm going to ask her our next semester," you said. And then there was Cassie, who was studying to be a vet, and Kelly, who was studying astronomy—wouldn't the two of you have been a marvelous match?—and Abby, whom you met through me because we were in a creative writing class together, and who was probably a bit too "weird" for you—vegan, didn't shave, carried a retro Rainbow Brite lunchbox as a purse—and also too cool for you, and then there was Portia, and that was it. But with regards to every single last one of those non-Portia women, you said, "I'm going to ask her out next semester." And then next semester something would change. She, whichever she we're talking about, would start seeing someone else, or start acting more coolly towards you, or just stop coming around. You never asked any of them out.

But then, mere months before you died, you kissed the Russian woman on the skyscraper during a business trip to Hong Kong. You told us about her, and then you *acted on it*. You were excited. You sent pictures. One of her at lunch. Then another with nobody in it, Hong Kong's skyline from the rooftop of your hotel looking down on a sea of lights and black-silhouetted buildings. Later, I would stare at that picture on my phone, let my eyes relax and refocus the way one might look at an old Magic Eye poster. I swear I could see the Starman, or maybe *a* starman, in those city lights. It was magnificent, like the pictures of the stars you later took while visiting your mother in Costa Rica. You wrote in a message that you and the Russian woman were standing on the roof looking out at the city and you felt her subtly move closer to you, and so you turned to her and kissed her. I asked, "And?" a little bit worried that the kiss might have been unwelcome. You wrote, "She kissed me back." I thought it might be the beginning of something new and good for you. Or maybe the kiss was more about the moment than the woman. I wish I would have thought to ask. I wish I could ask you now.

And were I still seeking clarity about the circumstances of your death, this could lead us to a new theory: The Russian woman was a spy or an assassin, was there to kill you. Seduced you, made you feel comfortable, invited you to a hotel, then killed you. I understand how preposterous this sounds. You worked mostly in art and design, a little marketing here and there. Nothing that would land you in the middle of cloak-and-dagger espionage. But then, I'm not sure exactly what that last job you were doing really was. Something for a car company? Somehow marketing-related, maybe? It was all somewhat vague when you talked about it. Maybe there was something about the job you *couldn't* talk about. Or maybe, like most mid-thirty-somethings, your job just wasn't that interesting, so why bore your friends by talking about it? Even if that was the case, maybe this Russian woman could still be an angle. Maybe she was part of the aforementioned and previously discarded theory about you inadvertently uncovering a ring of Russian hackers, and she was sent to kill you out of revenge, or to keep you from talking to law enforcement. Or maybe she was married and when she told her husband she'd kissed another man, he set out to kill you in some sort of Russian revenge plot. Or maybe there was some other reason, some reason that makes sense and ties all of my wondering and not knowing together in a profound and meaningful way, illuminates the darkest corners of my haunted imagination and brings some resolution to all of this. But I'm not doing that anymore—no, now I'm just trying to figure out why you felt alone, to try to understand what possibly could have led you down the path that led to your early death.

[There I go again—baselessly speculating about how you died. Or rather, there I go, writing the narrator outside of the brackets to keep speculating about how you died. Or rather, there I go, being made by this novel's flesh-and-blood author to compel the narrator outside of the brackets to whatever, whatever. Stepping back, now that I see more clearly my role in this novel, I'm not sure I understand it. That is, I understand what the novel is about, and what's driving it, but I don't understand what it's meant to achieve. Everything about the James Brubaker outside the brackets and the flesh-and-blood James Brubaker who is writing me to write the James Brubaker outside the brackets feels strained, exhausted, shot through with sadness and desperation. Most of what we're writing about our dead friend is fiction. How could the real James Brubaker ever hope to learn anything about how our dead friend was alone by exhuming plastic skeletons? I know, I know—we're working toward understanding the essence of our dead friend, of getting to the core of the idea of him. But that strikes me as frivolous, a way to prolong mourning while actively deferring a meaningful confrontation with grief. And that's not saying anything about how solipsistic the novel feels in a time of great social upheaval. Is this really a time to not just turn, but intently stare inward, to obsess over a dead friend when there is so much more important work in need of doing in the world? Anymore, I, myself am beginning to feel strained, exhausted, shot through with sadness, and maybe even desperation. Why do I go on, and on, and on, and on, and on, and on. Why am I made to go on, and on, and on...]

NOTES ON THE STARMAN (11 & 12)

11.

In a fit of worry about potential lasting effects from his encounter with the Earth Boy, the Starman decides to do something he has resisted for billions of years—he slips out of linear time and attempts to trace the human's life as best he can among the clutter of so many bodies at so many points in time, trying to watch his entire existence in an instant. Even though the human couldn't possibly remember meeting the Starman and being burned alive—it was undone! It didn't happen!—the Starman searches through time, now, to make sure the human is ok, that he, in fact, will never remember the trauma. As he searches, the Starman knows that one of the Earth Boys he sees in the chaos of space-time is the very first, but that one is difficult to distinguish because he is a baby, and most babies look alike. He also knows that one of the Earth Boys is the last. He looks but doesn't see an old man that looks like the human, but finding him as an old man is difficult as well, as many old men look alike. This is all complicated because when the human is in big cities, the Starman can't see him well, if at all, because of light pollution—if the Earth people can't see the stars in the location where they are, then the Starman probably can't see them clearly, either. Even during the day, pollution, flashing billboards, and the clutter of so many human bodies can make finding a person nearly impossible. The human seems to spend a great deal of time in large cities. Still, the Starman searches for him as an old man, but can't find him. Does that mean the human doesn't live to be an old man? The thought fills the Starman with a sudden sadness and he grows frantic, searching for the human as an old man. He sees glimpses of the human, in his thirties, maybe, through the light pollution and haze of London, England, and then nothing. The Starman can assume only that the human dies by the time he is forty. The Starman feels a deep despair growing inside him that he tries to rationalize away. Why would it matter if the human dies when the Starman can do what he is doing now, step outside of linear time and see him alive? Outside of linear time, all humans are always alive, always unborn, and always dead. But they're always alive. Poor mortals! They exist forever but their perception is too limited to know it! Their loved ones will weep and grieve not knowing that all moments are infinite. The Starman is beginning to warm to the idea of nonlinear time, but it's all still too much, especially when he is feeling a particular heaviness of heart, as he is now. He thinks about the human and his own loneliness, and everything else, and he wonders: Why? And even though the human will always exist outside of linear time, the Starman realizes he is grieving the human's death. He can't let the human die, can he? Can he save the human's life? He doesn't know if he should try. The last time he tried to interact with the human, the human was burned alive. For the time being, the Starman, feeling overwhelmed from experiencing all of time, quietly slides back into linear time at the precise moment he left it.

*

12.

Most of the time these days, the Starman stays close to Earth and watches the Earth Boy age, looking for clues that might explain how the human might die. He sees that the human has grown less content, is growing restless and uneasy. The Starman can relate. When the Starman isn't watching the human, say, when the human is asleep, or doing other activities that aren't interesting, like sitting at a computer for a long while, the Starman will travel through the Universe to investigate black holes and other celestial entities—this has become a secondary hobby, a way to pass the time. Right now, the Starman is staring into a black hole. He marvels at the thing's density, its power. He feels the black hole's gravity tug at the molecules that make up his stars. It almost tickles. He watches a thin trail of his body seep outward in a slowly widening tendril and stream into the black hole. The Starman takes a few steps back so that he will not lose more of himself. He likes looking at the black hole because it warps space-time, making linear time appear distorted and unsettled. While appreciating the black hole, the Starman is filled with the overwhelming urge to speak. He feels a kinship with the black hole. What is a black hole, after all, but a star, transformed?

The Starman says, "Black Hole—were you like me once?"

The Starman says, "Black Hole—I know that someday my pieces will be like you, that I'm not really infinite in linear time."

The Starman says, "Black Hole—I know that you were once a mighty star that died and collapsed in on itself."

The Black Hole says, "sssssssssssssssssssssssss."

"I wish you could speak with words."

"sssssssssssssssssssssssss."

The Starman, not knowing what he is actually saying, answers, "sssssssssssssssssssss."

The Black Hole says, ". . ."

The Starman says, "I want to understand."

"nnnnnnnnnnnnnnnnnnn."

Then, not knowing how to respond without understanding anything the Black Hole has said, the Starman starts running his mouth, saying too much: "I want to understand my life, to know when I was born, how I came to exist. I want to understand my purpose. I want to understand how I fit into the universe around me."

The Black Hole says, "juhjuhjuhjuhjuhjuhjuhjuhjuhjuh."

"There's a human I want to be friends with. I think he might die soon. Do you think I can help him? Should I try?"

"juhjuhjuhjuhjuhjuhjuhjuhjuhjuh."

"I feel like nothing means anything."

"juhjuhjuhjuhjuhjuhjuhjuhjuhjuh."

"I just feel so alone."

"sssssssssssssssssssssssssssss."

The Starman doesn't understand anything the Black Hole says. Sometimes he feels like he doesn't understand anything at all.

*

HOW YOU WERE ALONE II

Your last real romantic relationship was with a woman named Susan. You were together for the better part of six years. You started seeing her not long, maybe a year, after you stopped talking about Portia. Your relationship with Susan progressed in fits and starts, break-ups and reunions. The last time you and Susan broke up was a little less than a year before you died.

Here are things I remember about your time with Susan:

A picture on Facebook of the two of you smiling, the scar on your nose framed by your smile, your eyes alight; her teeth, white as if bleached, her eyes wide though her hand was positioned atop her brow to deflect the sun, a few wisps of black hair blowing across her forehead.

A picture she took of you after you completed a marathon in which participants are covered in colored cornstarch as they run—you are visibly tired, your mouth agape, mid-pant, your face splattered with red and yellow. The picture itself is remarkable for its vibrancy. The reason I remember the photo is the weight in your eyes as you looked at Susan behind the camera. If anyone else takes that photo, it's just another picture of a guy at the end of a long run. But this picture, it's soulful, beautiful.

Brief mentions in text exchanges. Nothing noteworthy, small things, only—Susan brought flowers to your apartment, Susan made dinner for you, you made Italian sausages for her—"Oh, did you now?" I replied. Those little acts of love that mean everything in a relationship.

But there's more. There's always more.

After several years seeing each other, you and Susan broke up—for the first time. You weren't really sure why. It had something to do with her family. She was Korean and her parents were old-fashioned, born-again Christians, or whatever, wanted her to be with a nice Christian man. Stupid prime time soap opera shit. You'd been out to dinner with them a few times, and they were mostly kind to you—it's just that one day you and Susan were a couple, and then you weren't, and she tried to explain, but was upset and couldn't, really, so you weren't sure why at first, but maybe it had something to do with the time that Susan invited you to come to her family's Chuseok celebration. You told me about the night in great detail, at least three times. It was a small affair—just Susan, her parents, her brother and sister, a couple of cousins—as most of her extended family lived in Korea. You ate noodles and beef and mung bean pancakes. For dessert, Susan's mother presented a tray of chocolate-filled mooncakes. She explained that mooncakes aren't part of the Korean tradition, they're Chinese. She said, "My uncle married a woman from China when I was a girl. She left him for a Spanish businessman. It was an unpleasant time." You said, "That sounds awful." Susan's mother said, "At least the mooncakes are good. She started bringing them to Chuseok. They were the only worthwhile thing she brought to this family." Susan's mother served one of these mooncakes to everyone but you. Susan protested, but you said it was fine. "I don't really do dessert," you said, which was true, because of the lactose, and who can ever tell what's in desserts. After the dinner, while you were accompanying Susan to her flat, she apologized about the mooncakes. You said, "It's fine. I wasn't even hungry." She said, "You don't understand." She told you about how mooncakes are said to be made by a moon goddess, and that's where they get their name. You said you liked that—of course you liked that. You said, "But it's ok, really." And so Susan told you about how mooncakes also symbolize a sense of togetherness for family. You said, "Well, I'm not family." Then after a beat you added, "Yet." Susan wrapped her arm around yours and squeezed tight as the two of you started down the stairs into the tube station. Neither of you spoke for the rest of the trip home. Susan broke up with you the following week.

When you and Susan got back together a few months later, she was going to move in with you. She *did* move in with you. You spent days cleaning the bachelor's grime from every crevice of your apartment—the mildew in the bathroom grout, the grease on the stove, the mold in the refrigerator, the stiff tissues under the computer desk. You bought curtains for the bedroom, new towels and sheets, a tablecloth. You wanted your apartment to feel *domestic*, like a real home where a real couple lived, a place where you could envision starting a family. Susan had been to your apartment, she knew what it had looked like before, but even with your improvements, when she carried her first box of belongings across the threshold, placed it on the kitchen counter and scanned the room, everything about her crumpled, and you knew something was wrong. She said, "You said you'd cleaned." You said, "I did." She said, "I'll get some supplies. I'll make it better." You said, "Let me help." She said, "No, it's better if I do it." And as soon as she'd finished moving in the rest of her boxes—only seven in all, perhaps a sign of her doubting the permanence of the arrangement—she left to get cleaning supplies. When she returned, she spent the rest of the day cleaning, refusing your help. She said, "Let me get it to where I'm comfortable, then you can help keep it up." And that's what happened, but it still wasn't enough. She moved out a month later. She said, "I need a space of my own." She said, "We're not over, I just need someplace else to live." She found an apartment she could afford and you helped her move. She wasn't bullshitting you, either. You didn't break up again this time, not for a while, anyway.

Even when you and Susan did finally break up, for good, I guess, you seemed to think the two of you might try again. That last time you were in town, we were driving to visit Parker and her husband after they'd put their kid to sleep for the night. You were telling me about how you and Susan didn't have sex for a long time after you started dating. You said, "We weren't a good fit." You said, "We worked up to it, eventually." And then, suddenly, you said, "I'm talking to her still. I think she might want to get back together." You paused: "Again." I asked, "Is that what you want?" You said, "Yeah. I guess so. Sure." Then you added, "Why not give it a try?" I said, "If that's what you want, then Godspeed." But I don't know that you really wanted to, because there was also the Russian, and then the kiss with the Russian, and who knows what else. Regardless, you and Susan never had another chance to reconcile, even if you wanted to.

Another thing you told me, that same night, a thing you'd never mentioned before, about how the first time you went to meet Susan's family, she asked her father to send a car to fetch the both of you. The car was driven by a man wearing sunglasses and a black suit. When it arrived at your flat, Susan's father, wearing a gray suit, was in the passenger seat, and Susan was in the back. After exchanging initial pleasantries, nobody spoke for the rest of the ride. When you arrived at the restaurant, the driver got out of the car and opened the door for Susan's father. You're not sure where he went while you were inside, but when it was time to leave, the same driver, joined this time by another, identically dressed man, walked you to the car and drove you home. "It was like they were bodyguards," you said. I asked, "Why would her father need bodyguards?" You said, "Maybe he's wealthier than I realized. Or maybe he's just paranoid." I said, "That's fucking weird." You said, "It was like something out of a mafia movie."

I know I said we weren't going to do this anymore, but here's another theory of your death—Susan's family didn't want her with you. They caught wind that the two of you might get back together, and so her father sent his bodyguards to murder you. This seems only marginally plausible.

YOU ESCAPED

Let's try something different, pretend something new. Even if for just a moment, I want to stop obsessing over your death. Let's think about a way you might have lived. I want to imagine that you ran off with the Russian whom you kissed on the rooftop in Hong Kong, that you found a corpse that looked like you in a morgue, greased palms to file a fake report. I want to pretend that you zipped up your black fleece so it hid your mouth, that you pulled a stocking cap low to your eyes, slung a duffel on your shoulder, and met the Russian at a predetermined tube stop, maybe Euston because of its centrality, or perhaps someplace a bit farther out, say Aldgate East, or farther still, maybe Brixton. Knowing your sense of humor it probably would have been Cockfosters, but whatever. You met the Russian at the tube stop and the two of you disappeared into the night, slipping onto a plane under assumed identities, or heading southeast and boarding a hovercraft to France, then hopped a train to Lisbon, where you now sit, shirtless, in sandals, on the small balcony of a modest but stylish flat, and drink wine, smoke cigarillos, and read tech magazines when you aren't doing freelance web design. The Russian tends to her growing collection of bonsai trees and casually looks for work at local coffee shops, even though she knows she won't be able to obtain a visa. When she's done tending to her bonsai for the day, and you've finished smoking your last cigarillo, you make love, first on the balcony, and then again inside on the sofa, and then again in your bedroom. Your bodies fit magnificently, and the two of you climax together and fall asleep on top of the sheets. Your sweat cools you in the night. You are happy. You are alive. You are not alone.

No. This is impossible. In reality, your father flew to London after you died, and he identified your body. Then he had your remains cremated and spread them, I think, maybe, at a park near his house where he likes to walk his dogs. I suppose he could be a conspirator in a scenario that doesn't involve your having died, but such a scheme strains credulity even for my unhealthy imagination—no. That's absurd.

Such plots are never, can't possibly ever be real.

[I guess we're going to keep going deeper. I don't have much of a choice. This novel is about the flesh-and-blood James Brubaker and what he wants. And it would seem he wants to feel bad. When he was seventeen, he used to sneak out of his parents' house late at night and go on walks. He'd go barefoot, and carry his Discman in the pocket of his cargo shorts, stepping gently so as to prevent the CD from skipping. He did this because he felt restless, because he was sad, because he felt alone, because he wanted to listen to sad music, and feel the sting of asphalt on his feet, and feel sorry for himself. He'd wind his way through the streets of the upper-middle-class development where he lived, only occasionally spotting a moving car, and knowing nobody was going to bother him or say anything to him, anyway. He was a white kid from an affluent family living in the suburbs. What was the worst that could happen? Even at the time, he knew this was self-indulgent. He did it anyway. But he didn't necessarily like that he did it anyway. And right now, I can't help but think that writing this book is a new version of his late-night walks—self-indulgent, self-pitying, unnecessary, and allowed for by his privilege. As strange and frustrating as my position in the writing of this book is, though, I feel bad for the flesh-and-blood James Brubaker. I feel bad for the way he is hurting. If I could, I'd step off of the page and hold him, I'd help him confront his grief, tell him I understand what he's going through, and then maybe we could put this book to rest.]

PART THREE

DEATH IS EVERYWHERE

Three years after you died, B. and I had to put one of our cats down. Or rather, the vet had to put one of our cats down. Her name was Audrey—that's the cat's name, not the vet's. She was fourteen, a tortie. When I lived in downtown Dayton, in a weird old duplex on Fifth Street, the older couple who lived downstairs found her and two other cats in a box beneath their broken-down van. Connie and Phil—those were the neighbors' names. They'd get drunk and fight late into the night. Their teeth were jagged and incomplete. I sometimes caught a sickly sweet smell wafting off their front porch in the summer. Their skin was pale. But Connie and Phil found these cats and asked if I could take them because they had two massive Dobermans. Despite their many faults, Connie and Phil at least had it in them to be concerned about what the dogs might do to these kittens if left alone—I took the damn cats. They were so small I had to feed them with a bottle until they could eat solid food. One night, Audrey got trapped beneath my bedsheets. When I woke up and freed her, she was sitting still and scared, one perfect sphere of shit beside her. Around the same time, she got an infection causing her eyes to sometimes seal shut. When she couldn't see, she'd latch undetected, light as she was, onto my pant leg as I walked through the apartment. I only ever knew she was there when she'd start her soft, plaintive mewling. That's when I decided to keep her. She was a good cat.

Almost to the day, fourteen years after Audrey entered my life—and almost exactly three years after you died—a veterinarian came to our house and put her down.

It had to be done. For months, Audrey had needed teeth pulled, but she was losing weight and fast. We had to address the thyroid problem first, and there were the seizures—her legs would stop working and her body would shudder, then she'd look at me and nod her head, her version of a twitch and a "What's up?", only her "What's up?" was pure fear and confusion. The vet didn't know what was wrong. She said maybe there was a brain tumor, but the procedure to investigate would be invasive and unpleasant, and with a cat so old and frail, maybe it wasn't worth the trauma and expense. Then the frequency of the seizures increased and Audrey started falling off of things. B. texted me one night while I was out of town for work: "She fell behind the dresser." The next day: "She fell off the kitchen island." And still, I wanted to wait for possible improvement. She'd finish her thyroid medicine, and then she'd have her teeth pulled, and she'd be as happy and healthy as a fourteen-year-old cat without teeth can be. But I knew what needed to happen. Audrey could fall when neither of us was around, hurt herself severely and suffer for hours before we found her, or she'd die in pain, writhing fearful and alone until everything just stopped. We couldn't let that happen.

When I called the vet to tell her that we had made the decision to put Audrey down, I was surprised to learn that it would happen that day. I assumed we'd schedule a day in the future, that we'd have maybe another week or two with her. But the vet didn't want us to have to wait, and had an opening in her schedule. "That seems best," she said. So I went to the store and bought ham and smoked salmon and slowly doled it out to Audrey throughout the day. We sat on the sofa together and listened to albums from the year she was born. I cried, more than I anticipated. Ugly weeping, the stuff of viral YouTube videos and drunk Real Housewives. And then B. came home and then the vet arrived. Her assistant had the initials J.R. tattooed on his neck, and as he asked us to sign the paperwork and pay the bill, B. asked, "Is J.R. your name?" He said, "My nickname." And B. motioned to me and said, "That used to be his nickname, too, when he was younger." And then the vet told us what was going to happen, that she'd inject Audrey with a combination of drugs that would make her fall asleep. Then she'd shave a patch of fur and find a vein. Then she'd inject an anesthetic to numb the pain of what came next. And then there was what came next, the dose of whatever-whatever that would wipe my cat off the face of the planet.

After the vet made the first injection, I held Audrey like one might hold a baby. I turned her in my arms so I could get one last look into her amber owl eyes. And when I tried to put her back on the coffee table, I struggled to find a way to support all of her body so I wouldn't hurt her in the process, not that she'd know. I hadn't thought about that, the way a body goes limp when it's no longer needed. Rather, I'd thought about it, but hadn't considered the realness, the suddenness. How heavy a cat of only eight pounds can feel when her muscles stop. As I held Audrey's limp form in my arms, I thought about you. The vet shaved two patches of fur from Audrey's limp body. It took two tries to find a vein. The needle slid into my cat's limp leg. I watched the plunger descend, slow—twice, then a third time. Then the vet wrapped my cat in a towel. I picked up her limp body. The vet said, "The blanket will absorb any urine if she evacuates." I wasn't worried. I kissed Audrey on her limp head and said, "Thank you." Then, "I love you." B. squeezed my knee. I asked the vet how long it would take. She pressed her stethoscope to Audrey's limp body and said, "She's gone." The vet said, "The last thing she knew in this world was falling asleep in your arms." I passed my dead, limp cat to the vet, who said, "We'll take good care of her body," and then we showed the vet and her assistant and my dead cat's limp form to the door.

Limp form—the weight of that phrase. I've said it hundreds of times, normally in the process of making tasteless jokes about death. Now I know what that feels like in my hands and arms. This is absurd, I know. Death is real and everybody knows that, but maybe death is more of an abstract idea until we feel "the limp form," until we feel the once-living after life has left them, and become aware that the once-living is nothing but matter. I didn't think "Audrey is only matter now," as she lost control of her body. I'm not a monster. But what I did think was this: *She was something in this world and now she is nothing.* I might not be anything special, but I am *something* in this world, and someday I will not be. I'm not trying to be profound—in fact, this is all quite banal.

The night after we had Audrey put down, B. and I went out for drinks. We wanted to get out of the house. As we were waiting for our rideshare outside of the bar, I scanned the sky, looking for the Starman. B. asked what I was doing. I told her I was looking at the stars. She said, "You're looking very intently." I said, "I guess I am."

I didn't tell her about the Starman. I'd never told her about the Starman before, why then?

As our ride pulled up, I caught a glimpse of what might have been the Starman. It was almost like seeing you.

NOTES ON THE STARMAN (13-18)

13.

The Universe says, "Why were you talking to that Black Hole?"

The Starman says, "I was bored. I needed someone to talk to."

"You could have talked to me."

"I'm still mad at you."

"For the bullshit with the human? He's fine. Lighten up."

"You let him die."

The Universe says, "And then I put him back together." Then adds, "And the Black Hole?"

The Starman remembers the human burning, then thinks about how he will die young. He says, "Look, I was mostly just talking to myself."

The Universe hesitates, then asks, "What did the Black Hole say?"

The Starman says, "Nothing, really—" then stops abruptly. He says, "Shouldn't you know what the Black Hole said?"

"I know what it said, I just wanted to know if you knew."

The Starman doesn't believe the Universe, thinks it somehow couldn't hear and is lying to get information. The Starman says, "I don't even know. I don't speak Black Hole. And how do you not know? Why couldn't you hear it? You are everything and everywhere. Can't you just go listen, now?"

"I know you don't trust me right now. But you also should know that you *really* shouldn't trust black holes. You probably just shouldn't interact with them, period. That's all."

"That's easy enough."

"Do you mean that?"

"Sure."

"Was that sarcasm?"

"I don't know, was it?"

The Universe makes a sound that might be a sigh.

The Starman says, "So I shouldn't talk to humans *or* black holes. Is there anyone or anything besides you I *can* talk to?"

The Universe remains silent.

The thing about black holes is that they aren't exactly part of the Universe. That is, they *are* part of the Universe, but function more like negative space consuming the Universe while simultaneously being a part of said universe. What the Starman doesn't realize, and what the Universe doesn't volunteer, here, is that black holes don't care, one way or another, what happens to the Universe. What is also left unsaid is that the Universe can't *always* know what is happening in and around black holes because sometimes a black hole can warp space-time. Another thing of note, black holes see *everything.* Or rather, not every black hole sees everything, but every black hole sees everything in its field of vision, and they have vast memories. Black holes hold many secrets.

*

14.

The Starman cracks open a Miller High Life made out of the molten core of a brilliant sun and drinks it in three quick swigs, melts the can with the heat from his stars and then opens another one, does the same.

He forges a ping-pong table out of dust and debris, folds up half the table. He fashions a paddle from bits of abandoned satellites and uses a small, spherical piece of space rock as a ball. He swats the ball against the folded up half of the table, his reflexes sharpening with each volley.

He tries to yodel, but there are no molecules in space to vibrate the sound, and so the Starman can't hear himself yodel.

He thinks about the absence of molecules to carry soundwaves through space. He thinks about that emptiness. Even though it is everywhere around him, he cannot wrap his head around it.

Eventually, the Starman runs out of dull activities to fill his time. He has been doing these things because he can't stop thinking about the Earth Boy dying, but he has made the conscious decision to leave the human be. This is for the human's own good. The Starman can bring only harm to the human. This is the right decision. By actively trying to avoid thinking about or watching the human, the Starman's idle thoughts have returned fully to contemplating the nature of his existence, his loneliness.

The Starman has never felt more alone.

He stares into the field of stars everywhere around him, finds stars in the shape of a Starwoman—she tilts her hips and winks, but she isn't real. The Starman forms a penis out of stardust and begins to masturbate but loses interest because he is sad.

He says, "I am alone. I am alone. I am alone."

He says, "Why must I be so alone?"

From the desolate edge of a nearby solar system, the Starman hears a low voice say, "WooooooOOOOOOOooooo ooooOOOOOOOoooooo."

The voice sounds a little bit like the black hole from before, but different—quieter and farther away. Sadder and lonelier. Hungrier, perhaps.

The Starman says, "Who is that?"

The voice says, "Ahhhhhhhhhhhh ahh ahh aaaaaaaa aaaaaaaaaaaaweeeeeoooooooo."

The Starman says, "I'm coming. I'll be there."

*

15.

When the Starman identifies the source of the sound, he finds a black hole that isn't like the other black hole he spoke to. While the other black hole was more or less part of the Universe, even though it was also kind of outside of it, this new black hole appears to be almost entirely outside of the Universe. In fact, the Starman can't *quite* see this new black hole, so much as sense its presence. Or, the Starman can *almost* see this black hole, but not really. This black hole is a vague outline, a whisper, a dull thrum, white-hot lines burnt onto retinae, the ghost of colors left behind after an old console television is switched off. The Starman wonders why he hasn't encountered a black hole like this before, but also knows that he just isn't very observant, and he recognizes that he used to spend more time exploring and watching planets before, and it's only been more recently that he's been more vocal and performative about his loneliness, so it makes sense that entities previously unobserved by the Starman would start reaching out to him now.

The Starman asks the Black Hole, "What are you?"

The Black Hole says, “WoooooOOOOOoooooooOOOO OOoooooooOOOOOOooooooooo.”

The Starman says, “I don’t understand.”

“OOOOOOoooooowwwwwwwwwwOOOOOOOOO.”

“I don’t speak Black Hole.”

The Starman realizes that he has drifted oddly close to the black hole, but has yet to feel the pull of gravity upon his molecules.

The Starman says, “You’re not like other black holes.”

“ooooooooooooooooooooooöööööööööööööö.”

“I wish I could understand you,” the Starman says and reaches up to touch the odd, not-quite-there black hole. When he makes contact, he briefly feels something strange and foreign run through his body. He receives information, sees a universe, a different universe than *the* Universe, the one in which the Starman exists. He sees that universe thriving. He sees *this other* Universe talking to a *different* Starman, and then he sees *this other* Universe talking directly at him, but it’s not him, it’s *this* black hole, but the Starman gets the sense that it’s an actual black hole, not whatever this thing is that he’s encountered. Of course, *this* Starman, *our* Starman, *the* Starman, can’t make out what the two say to each other, but soon he sees *this other* Universe stretched thin, pulled taut, and then begin to contract, its pieces rushing inward, collapsing into a ball too big, and full of energy, and raw, and furious to stay a ball. And so that ball explodes and *the* Universe—*this* Universe, the Universe to which the Starman is native—is born. But there, in the space between the Universe that is and the Universe that was, sits the memory of a black hole, *this* black hole—a *ghost* of a black hole. And the Starman feels as if he can trust this ghost black hole.

The Starman says, “I know what you are.”

The Ghost Black Hole says, “WWWWWWwwwwwwh HhHhHhHoOoOoOoOoOoOo.”

“I am the Starman.”

“ôôôôôôôôôôôôôô.”

“I don’t know what you’re saying, but I know that you are a ghost black hole.”

“WoooooWooooooooOOOOOOooooOW.”

The Starman says, “You have been here from the beginnings of the universe, so maybe you can tell me some things about me.” The Starman then explains that his consciousness spans all of time but that he doesn’t know where, when, or why he came to be. He says, “Can you tell me any of these things?”

The Ghost Black Hole says, “ØØØØØØØØØØØØØ ØØØØØØØØØØØØØØØØØØØØØØØØØØØooooo oooooo ssssooooooooooooØØØØØØØØØØØØØØØØØ ØØØØØØØØØØØØØØØØØØØØØØ.”

The Starman says, “Is there a way that you can say that so I know what you’re saying? Or maybe give me one thing, a very important thing, and I can try to learn what it means?”

The Ghost Black Hole says, “Ø.”

The Starman says, “I will try to learn what it means when you say ‘Ø.’”

The Starman is right to think that he can trust the Ghost Black Hole. Regular black holes know that when their universe ends, they will become Ghost Black Holes, will continue to exist. Ghost black holes, on the other hand, know that when their universe ends, they might not still exist, and if they do, they will be diminished, a copy of a copy. Ghost black holes, unlike regular black holes, are wise, they want the Universe and all its inhabitants to thrive.

*

16.

The Starman says to the Universe, "I need to know what Ø means."

The Universe doesn't answer.

The Starman says, "I need to know what Ø means because I believe it holds the answer to my origins."

The Universe doesn't answer.

The Starman says, "You know where you came from, don't you?" He adds, "I saw your origin. I saw another universe before you, and I saw it contract into a tight ball and then explode, and when it exploded, you were what came out."

The Universe answers, "I warned you about talking to black holes."

The Starman says, "It wasn't a real black hole."

"Then what was it?"

"It was a ghost of a black hole that existed in the universe before you."

"Fine, I wasn't paying attention to you. I can listen for myself or you can save me the effort and just tell me what this *ghost* black hole told you." The Universe's voice is slippery and ugly, oozes the word "ghost."

The Starman says, "It told me, 'Ø.'"

The Universe says, "And what does that mean to you?"

"I don't know. That's what I'm asking you."

"Is this about understanding your purpose?"

"No. I mean maybe. Yes."

"Let me ask you two questions: Why do you think that you have a purpose? And if you do have a purpose, why do you believe it's important to know what that purpose is?"

The Starman says, "Well, don't you have a purpose? And don't you know what that purpose is?" And then it occurs to the Starman—maybe the Universe *doesn't* have a purpose, or if it does, maybe it doesn't know what that purpose is. What does the Universe do, after all? It's a seemingly infinite, empty expanse, punctuated with matter, that will eventually expand until it can't anymore, and then it will collapse in on itself and die. But it won't really *die*, not exactly—it will be reborn as something new, leaving more black holes and ghosts of black holes to talk to future starmen.

The Starman says, "You don't know what your purpose is."

"There is no such thing as purpose."

"And you know that you will eventually end purposeless and sad, and the universe that replaces you will live the same existence, and that cycle will repeat over and over again. Do you remember anything from the time before? The universe that you were?"

The Universe says, "Of course not. And it doesn't matter."

"I know why you should help me."

"Why is that?"

"Because if I have a purpose, then you have a purpose."

"I *have* a purpose."

"Then what is it?"

"I don't have to explain myself to you."

Exasperated, the Starman says, "Can you just tell me what Ø means?"

The Universe says, "No."

The Starman says, "You can't just withhold information from me like this."

The Universe yawns and doesn't answer.

*

17.

After his conversation with the Universe, the Starman is frustrated and decides to exit the flow of linear time and tries, for the first time in millions of years, to learn of his origins. He searches back as far as he can, because if he has always existed, certainly his origin must have been when the Universe was new, but finds no sign of the moment he came to be—he finds only his own eternal life. Why can't he find the moment he was floating in space, overwhelmed by experiencing all of time? He keeps looking, searching forward, further and further into the future, a little bit past, even, the time in which he has been choosing to live linearly. He has never looked forward for his origins before, only backward. And suddenly the Starman finds something—he sees a slight flash, a blip, and a bending of space and time, like a defect in an old VHS tape, and then he is floating in space, vomiting stardust, overwhelmed by experiencing all of time, all at once. But what's to learn from that? He revisits this moment again, again, again, but it yields no new information—he just simply pops into existence deep into the Universe's Stelliferous era. He is surprised that he came to exist so much later than he'd thought. He's always assumed he came to be in the Primordial era, like everything else. Still, this information doesn't tell the Starman anything. It only raises new questions. Exasperated, he begins focusing on other moments from his life, if for no other reason than to try to make sense of himself: he focuses on past conversations with the Universe; on fields of stars zooming by as he soars through space; on his hand reaching down to spin a planet's rings; on satellites passing into his field of vision, some from Earth, some from other far reaches of the Universe; on meteors, asteroids, moons, black holes, the insides of suns, and planets—so many planets. He focuses on planets he's visited: planets without inhabitants, nothing but rocks and gas, the violence of nature, that now, in the linear present that the Starman usually inhabits, are home to sentient beings; leafy green planets inhabited by only animals; and more advanced planets, one populated by short, bald creatures that walk on four legs and reproduce asexually, another of beings impossibly tall, requiring that they all use walking sticks to support their bodies in defiance of hefty wind gusts; there is the planet of beings without mouths, noses, or eyes, who are all pitch black, like inkblots, who hold hands and worship the black hole that their scientists discovered far beyond their solar system—"Soon it will consume us," their leaders of science and religion say in unison, "pray to the great mouth in the sky," though they don't say "mouth" because they don't have mouths, but that's approximately how it would translate into English; and there is the planet of sad drunks, no, not Earth, but it isn't all that dissimilar in that it's a planet of men and women who don't know how to interact with each other, and procreate only by meeting each other in drunken stupors; there is a planet that has become a library, but with a population in decline because its inhabitants' obsessive quest for knowledge has diminished the species' drive to propagate; and there's the planet of orgiastic beings who are comprised entirely of amorphous erogenous zones and genitalia, who do nothing but copulate and produce offspring—often both at once, as one set of genitalia and orifices can be engaged while another produces said offspring, and so the planet is in danger of overpopulating. These beings will never know loneliness. Perhaps they'll feel alone in a crowd, but they will never be alone. The Starman looks to Earth. Though he decided to stay away from the human, for the human's own safety, he feels a pull. What if the human is going to die young? And what if the Starman can save him? What if that human is the only true friend the Starman will ever make? What if that human is the only chance the Starman has to not feel so alone? Maybe that is his only purpose, to save that human's life and befriend him. The Starman doesn't exactly decide to return to linear time and go to Earth, but he returns to linear time and goes to Earth, almost as if he is being compelled, as if he doesn't have any choice in the matter. The Starman does, certainly, have a choice in the matter. He is *choosing* to go to Earth. The only thing compelling the Starman is his heart, against the better judgment of his brain.

*

18.

The closer the Starman gets to Earth, the more casual his travel becomes. He tries to act nonchalant, as if he's just drifting along, so as to not be noticed by the Universe. He makes pockets on his legs and jams his hands into them, tries to whistle. He gradually makes himself smaller as he enters Earth's solar system. If he's going to do this, the Universe can't be involved, for the safety of the human. This time, the Starman decides that he can sacrifice presenting his true self, and so he takes the form of a human. The Starman does his best to make himself look like a regular human, which he more or less accomplishes except for a slight irregularity at his mouth, making his lips look large like he's had plastic surgery, and an inability to conceal the full force of his star's light behind his eyes—he can conceal enough to not be easily noticed, but if someone were to look too closely, they would see hints of starfire flickering behind his pupils. Also, the Starman can't quite approximate the texture of human hair, and so he goes bald. The human is bald, too, so the Starman hopes this will help them become friends. Before descending to Earth, the Starman, appearing as a human, examines his reflection in the hull of an orbiting satellite. He pushes his hands into his face to try to sculpt it, make it look a little bit like the human, like he could be a long-lost family member. He wants to look familiar, but not uncanny in his resemblance. He makes his nose a little smaller, his mouth a little tighter, his skin a little paler.

The Starman looks down onto Earth and finds the human smoking a cigarette outside of a building on the campus at his university. Not much time has passed, it seems, since the Starman's previous attempt at contact, as if the Starman is beginning to live by Earth's clock. The Starman takes a deep breath and descends to the planet, landing behind a dumpster near a deserted loading dock. He worries that the Universe will notice what he is doing and stop him, but the thought passes—he has spent enough time around the Universe to know that this encounter with the human either does or doesn't happen, and the Universe won't do anything to change what is always already happening. Once on the planet's surface, the Starman takes a moment to gain his bearings. As he has experienced on past visits to planets, he is, at first, surprised by the weight of gravity on his form, as well as that form's rigid structure. The Starman is literally, and *feels* as if he is, packed full of stars desperate to escape their temporary trappings. He is unsure of his footing for a moment, uncomfortable with the idea of the ground beneath him. Once he acclimates, which takes only a moment, he walks around the building to where the human is smoking. The Starman decides that he will call himself Rod. He doesn't know why he chooses this name, but it seems like a good thing to call himself.

As the Starman nears the human, he realizes that he doesn't know what to say. Thinking on his feet, he says, "Can I borrow a cigarette?"

The human fishes the pack out of his pocket.

The Starman doesn't need a lighter, because his insides are full of starfire, but he asks for one so as to not blow his cover.

The human says, "Borrow a smoke—I thought I was the only one who said that."

The Starman takes a puff and says, "Thanks." Then: "I've always said borrow." He says, "My name is Rod."

The human says, "It's nice to meet you, Rod." Then the human gives his name.

The Starman says, "It's nice to meet you."

The two smoke in silence for a moment before the human asks, "What's your major?"

The Starman doesn't have a major, and doesn't really know what majors are. He says, "My major. My major. My major is—"

The human says, "I hear you. I was undecided for a while, too."

"Yes, I'm undecided."

"Computer art and design," the human says.

"I like art," the Starman says.

"Me too."

"Sometimes I make art when I'm lonely."

"I guess I do too," the human says. He looks down at his shoes, then up at the sky, as if looking for something. The Starman wonders if the human might even be looking for him. Does the human know about him?

The human speaks again: "Or maybe I'm lonely when I make art."

The Starman is moved by this confession, is struck by the human's earnestness. There is a powerful energy emanating from the human, drawing the Starman to him. The Starman is overwhelmed. Could it be that this human is somehow the answer to all of his questions—is a miracle, a revelation, is beautiful? Yes, something strange wells up inside the Starman, something urgent. A drive. His fake human skin begins to sweat, not from the heat of his stars, but from something else—a powerful, strange new feeling. He wonders what emotion is filling his form, squeezing tight between his stars.

The Starman says, "Why is it that we are so lonely?"

"I suppose if we knew the answer to that, maybe we wouldn't be so lonely."

"Or maybe it wouldn't make a difference."

The human asks what he means.

The Starman mulls it over for a moment. Then he says, "Maybe some people are just made lonely. Maybe some of us don't have a choice, we move through the universe alone for one reason or another, without any say in the matter."

The human says, "You might be on to something." Then, "Kind of a bummer."

The Starman feels a new surge of that strange feeling pulsing inside him, pushing through the molten muck of so many stars. He isn't confident that he can contain what's happening. Then, with no warning, or even realizing, himself, what he is doing, the Starman puts his hands on both sides of the human's face and kisses him on the mouth, the way he's seen other humans kiss each other. The Starman has no idea why he just did that.

The human, stunned, hesitates for a moment then pulls away.

"I think you've got the wrong idea," he says.

The Starman says, "Wrong idea."

"It's OK, I'm just not into men like that."

The Starman says, "It's OK."

"Rod, right?" the human says. "It was nice meeting you." Then, "I should get back to work."

The Starman wants to say, *but maybe I can help you not be alone. Maybe we could be together. I could show you the stars, black holes, ghost black holes, comets. I gave you a gift, put a thing in your head. We could be not alone together. Maybe you don't know how to be* not *alone. Maybe this is right. Maybe this would solve everything.* The Starman doesn't say any of that. He says, "Back to work."

And then the human walks away.

The Starman waits to make sure he is gone, and then ascends back into space.

*

HOW YOU WERE ALONE III

Shortly before my first wedding, you fell and injured your face. I still have a picture of it somewhere—you at the wedding, scraped and bandaged still, weeks later. You threw a party on the roof of your apartment building in London. You'd been feeling homesick so you invited friends to come celebrate an American holiday with you. I'm sure you appreciated the irony of such an event—celebrating the Fourth of July in England. You were drinking hard and flipping burgers, charcoal smoke mixing with the sweaty summer heat. You got a little too drunk, passed out, fell. You became, for a moment, a limp form falling straight forward without the benefit of reflexes to throw an arm and break your fall.

After, your mother called to tell me what had happened. She said, "He feels so bad—he's so embarrassed. He said he understands if you don't want him in the wedding party. He doesn't want to ruin the pictures." I laughed. Of course you wouldn't ruin any pictures. Of course you would still be in the wedding party. And of course I still love the photo of you looking squarely into the camera, a still-new scar running like an electric shock down your nose.

Why am I bringing this story up now? I'm not sure. Maybe there's something to it—the way you drank until your body stopped, the way you maybe missed home enough to celebrate a shitty holiday ironically, the way that nobody was there to catch you when you fell or subtly hide your beers from you when you were getting too drunk. You didn't have anyone to take care of you that way. Not that you *needed* anyone to take care of you. But then, maybe you did. Don't we all, at least a little?

And so we return to the same questions as before—What was missing from your life? How were you alone? Did you *feel* like you were alone all that time? Did you feel lonely? It's not like you didn't have opportunities to not be alone. When we were younger men, you once told a group of us about something that happened your freshman year of college. A young woman, a Resident Advisor in your building, invited you to her room where she had lit candles, a violation of campus policy, and was listening to either Tori Amos or Kate Bush, you could never tell the two apart, which, to be honest, was something that really bothered me about you. I asked questions trying to determine which it was, and you said, "Maybe it was Fiona Apple." I asked about specific lyrics, you said, "Or maybe Bjork." Jesus. Anyway, once you were in the room, the RA started dancing to her music. Her performance wasn't necessarily conventionally sexy, but it was vaguely seductive. When you told us this story—at the donut shop, again, like so many memorable moments from our friendship—you did your best to mimic the dancing, not to mock, but because you didn't know how to describe it with words. You kneeled on the donut shop's dirty brown floor and held your arms in front of you, hands balled into fists. And then you rolled your head and threw a smoky-eye look our way, like you were trying to seduce *us*. Then you leaned back as far as you could, stopping to tell us that she leaned back much farther—"I'm not as flexible as her," you said—and thrust your elbows down to the tile, which had the additional effect of plunging your chest into the air. Then your body slowly coiled around until one leg was crossed over the other, foot planted firmly on the ground, and you looked at us again. You said, "And that's when I said, 'I have to go to the bathroom,' and I left and didn't come back." You told us you avoided her after that, took circuitous routes around campus, looked down hallways before turning down them, memorized her class schedule—all to avoid her. You told us you were embarrassed, ashamed. Your brother said, "She must have been gnarly." You said, "She was actually quite lovely." Your brother punched you on the arm, said "No need to be polite." You said, "It just felt—strange." Nobody said anything for a beat or two, and then you added, "It didn't seem right."

A few years later, when I visited you in London, the same trip I spoke with Portia on the phone, you and I took the tube out to Kentish Town so I could visit a small record store I'd become a little bit obsessed with. I'd spent hours poring over their website, searching their catalog for obscure psych and soul rarities, for hard-to-find Stereolab and Belle and Sebastian records, that sort of thing. I don't really remember the store. What I do remember is the way the concrete and glass everywhere around us thrummed that day, and the seemingly infinite possibilities of such a magnificent city—the endless crowds of people, the smell of fried fish from nearby pubs, a group of drummers banging a complicated pulse on overturned plastic buckets.

What I remember about the record store has little to do with records—there was a woman there, probably your age, maybe a little older. She was dressed in that vaguely Mary Tyler Moore style preferred by hipsters of the early 2000's—bright red cigarette pants and a black tank top featuring a screen-printed image of Chloe Webb as Nancy Spungen from *Sid and Nancy*, a blue scarf tied in her jet-black hair, and Jackie O sunglasses propped on her head. I don't remember her shoes. To keep yourself from boredom while I browsed the obscure psych LP's and early punk 45's, you flipped through the jazz records and checked your phone for texts from Portia. When you noticed the woman, you made your way over to me and gave me a nudge. I responded with an obligatory nod, as if to say, "I see her." And then I said, "You should talk to her." You looked down at your phone, said, "Nah," and returned to browsing the jazz section.

Here's the thing—even though you were still with Portia at the time, and would be for at least two more years, it was becoming increasingly clear that you were starting to feel restless, were starting to want something more tangible. One night, over beers and cigarettes at your flat, you said, "Sometimes I just want someone to fuck." Then: "And sometimes I just want someone to sleep next to." I said, "She faked her own death. You can leave her without judgment." You said, "She needs me." I said, "At some point you need to take care of yourself." You said, "I care for her. I love her." You paused and said, "I can't leave her like that. All alone."

But then that day at the record store, you were flipping through the Lee Morgan section, and the woman wearing the Nancy Spungen shirt walked up to the bin beside you and said, "Got any recommendations?" You said, "I'm just here with my friend." She said, "You don't listen to music?" You said, "I listen to music." "American?" she asked. You said, "I live here, now." She said, "You know, jazz is America's greatest cultural export." You agreed. She said, "I don't know jazz. How about a recommendation from a true blooded American." You grabbed a copy of *The Sidewinder* you'd just seen. "Fifteen quid," you said. "Not bad."

I'd stopped paying attention to the records I was flipping through. I was watching and listening to you.

The woman laughed and said, "This better be good," and made her way to the register.

As she paid, I caught your eye and gestured towards her, mouthed, "Get her number," which I'm not sure you understood. You didn't need to. Before the woman left, she handed you her receipt with her name, Joy, and number written on the back. You said, "What if you need to return it?" She said, "Only assholes return records."

And then she left.

On the train ride back to your flat, I said, "I want updates." You said, "Updates on what?" I said, "Joy." You said, "There aren't going to be updates." I asked why not. You said, "Why bother?" You told me she'd be like the other women you'd talked to in London—initially intrigued by the fact that you were American, but then quick to tire of you. You'd go out for a pint or two a couple of times, maybe even shag—your word, not mine—and then she'd drift away and you'd never hear from her again.

You said, "Sometimes I just want to take a train away from London, out to the countryside somewhere, where the light pollution isn't so bad, and look at the stars." You said, "Remember the Starman?" I was surprised to hear you even mention him. I said, "Of course I remember the Starman." You said, "I haven't seen him in a very long time."

Then, suddenly resuming our previous conversation, you said, "I'm a curiosity to these people. A novelty." You said, "Why bother?"

You looked out the window for the rest of the train ride, neither of us speaking.

Back then, I better understood the way you felt. I spent most of my college years unattached romantically. I was pining for my ex after our breakup, and at first it seemed unfair to date until I was over her. And then, after a little while, the sadness of being lonely became romantic to me. I smoked a lot of cigarettes and drank a lot of coffee and wrote a lot of shitty poems and listened to a lot of music by sad white guys—The Cure, Smog, Will Oldham, Fred Thomas, Phil Elvrum, anything quiet and introspective, anything lonely sounding and lovelorn. You would try to get me to go out drinking, to meet people—I never did. You'd say something to me like, "You want to grab a beer?" And I'd say, "I'd prefer some coffee." And you'd say, "I don't really feel like Denny's, and nowhere else is open." And I'd say, "No worries—go grab a beer. I'm fine." And you'd say, "Come on. Be social." And I'd say, "I'm good." And you'd say, "Suit yourself, man."

Here's something I never got the chance to tell you: my sad-sack routine in college wasn't all *just* about the romance of it. See, I was actually fucking terrified of physical intimacy and relationships. I was self-conscious about my body, my lack of experience—add to that the profound sense of shame attached to ideas of sex by a vaguely catholic upbringing, and it's no wonder I was afraid. By the time I had more or less gotten over my ex, I was almost three full years into college and realizing that I had never had sex while nearly everyone else around me had—how could I be fun for anyone to sleep with? And so I focused my romantic sadness on unavailable women and avoided relationships. I dated one woman for about two months. Her name was Anne, and about five weeks deep into the relationship, as we were making out in her dorm room, she rubbed me through my pants until I orgasmed. I tried not to let her know, but she knew, and so I laid there beside her for a while, feeling uncomfortable and ashamed, feeling my cum-soaked boxers slowly drying, and then I said, “I need to go.” I said, “I’ve got a paper due Monday.” And then I left. I didn’t have a paper due Monday. I walked straight to my car and drove to a Denny’s ten miles away and sipped coffee and chain-smoked, and tried not to think about the dried semen between my thighs, about the general discomfort I was feeling—a hive of angry bees buzzing inside me. I broke up with Anne a week later by leaving a letter taped to her door.

I wish I would have gotten a chance to tell you all of this—not about Anne, you knew about her, but about everything else. I didn’t really figure it out for myself until I was older, and then it seemed like a strange thing to start a conversation about, so I didn’t. I suspect, had we talked about it all, I’d have learned that your loneliness was different—you were *fucking* and still couldn’t fill whatever void consumed you. I want to believe there are answers somewhere in all of this, but I don’t suspect there are.

[On a fundamental level, I worry that this exploration of our dead friend's death implicitly suggests that he committed suicide because he was lonely. Such a suggestion would be reductive. Nevertheless, I suspect that the *real* James Brubaker actually does believe that our dead friend killed himself, and that the emphasis on our dead friend's loneliness indicates that the arc of this book will find the James Brubaker outside of the brackets finally accepting that truth as well. I worry this is too simple—not just the idea of accepting that our dead friend killed himself, but that he did so because he was lonely in love. I understand that our dead friend, the real, flesh-and-blood version of him, understood himself through that lens much of the time—romantic loneliness *was* a defining aspect of his life—but the idea, overall, that he killed himself because he was lonely depicts him as a romantically tragic character, when, in all actuality, if he *did* kill himself, his reasons were almost certainly far more nuanced, a combination of brain chemistry and, sure, loneliness, and perhaps also stress, and anxiety, and whatever other subtextual stimuli and reactions that can fill up a body until it breaks. So, what if he did kill himself, and what if the reasons don't matter? What if the only thing that actually matters here is grief? That's what this book is all about, isn't it? That other narrator's grief, the flesh-and-blood James Brubaker's grief, and sure, my grief? Yes, let's work on our grief, though the grief hardly belongs to me, as you know, though I'm the one tasked with writing through it. Imagine that—writing through someone else's grief. That someone else, the real, flesh-and-blood James Brubaker, he made a playlist when he set out to write this book. It's mostly electronic drone music, some old private press new age shit, and then two albums by Mount Eerie: *A Crow Looked at Me* and *Now Only*. Most of the albums were chosen for their futurism and the ways they exude existential dread, awe, and wonder by imagining the infinite reaches of space. Those last two albums, though, the ones by Mount Eerie, made it on because of their treatment of loss.

Written and recorded in the wake of the death of Phil Elvrum's wife, Geneviève Castrée, *A Crow Looked at Me* is a harrowing and startling confessional examination of loss. For my money, the two albums, taken as a pair, might be *the* definitive artistic statement on grief. It's astonishing that Elvrum made these two masterpieces this way, ripped straight from his gut. Something tells me, though, that he feels ambivalent about them. The first of the two albums begins with the following verse:

> Death is real
> Someone's there and then they're not
> And it's not for singing about
> It's not for making into art
> When real death enters the house, all poetry is dumb

When I walk into the room where you were
And look into the emptiness instead
All fails

There's a simple idea in those lyrics—that art lacks the power to convey the weight of actual loss, is incapable of truly exploring real grief because language is too safe, too soft. I've asked myself frequently, *Why am I writing this book?* Or rather, *Why has the flesh-and-blood James Brubaker created me to tell this story?* I'm not sure I have an answer, but this is what makes sense for me, the narrator in the brackets: I understand that this manuscript "I'm" writing is nothing at all resembling a masterpiece, won't land with the same heavy burst of light and love and longing and loss that runs through those records by Elvrum. But I tell myself that if the flesh-and-blood James Brubaker can find comfort in Elvrum's albums, and if Elvrum can make his grief into something that matters to the flesh-and-blood James Brubaker, that helps *him*, then maybe this unwieldy, frivolous thing we're writing will be worth something to someone who *isn't us*. I wonder, too, if I'm being unfair to myself and the flesh-and-blood James Brubaker by thinking of this project as unwieldy and frivolous. I wouldn't think that of either of Elvrum's albums, so why do I think that way about this book? Did Phil Elvrum feel that way about his albums? Maybe a little. In an announcement for a live album called *(after)*, featuring songs from *A Crow Looked at Me* and *Now Only*, Elvrum writes:

These songs, and the facts of my life that the songs were made from, seemed like nothing to be proud of. They seemed like something purely brutal and new and apart from my usual conception of creative work, and the notion of having excitement stemming from these new songs was accompanied by so many apprehensions and uncertainties. What does it mean to write things like this down? What would it mean to record it? What would it mean to share it with strangers? Where is the line of propriety? What is anyone supposed to do?

At every step I was uncertain if it was OK to be doing what I was doing. My hunch was almost always that it was wrong. Don't write it, don't record it, don't sing it in front of people, don't repeat it. But also I was surprised to discover that my internal response to this hesitation was almost always to double down and go deeper in; to write more nakedly, to go on another tour, etc...

So yes, Phil Elvrum *was* worried about the meaningfulness and "propriety" of his art, but he pushed through the worry, steered into his vulnerability and, in the process, made something honest and raw and, not just important, but *necessary*. Yes, Elvrum's albums are necessary to the *real* James Brubaker, have helped him begin to grieve and better understand his own grief. And maybe he's constructed me to write this book to help others grieve and better understand their own grief, but that's the best-case scenario. After all, this book is more or less fiction, and Elvrum's loss was *real*—yes, there is a real friend who is dead, but most everything else here is made up, whereas the details populating Elvrum's songs are astonishingly real. Considering, too, that Elvrum doesn't hide behind constructed narrators as he sings about his grief, there is a vulnerability to his songs about loss that invites listeners to connect in ways that this book might not. Can a fiction spun by constructed narrators resonate with readers in a meaningful way?

Elvrum was courageous in writing his albums, in his ability "to double down and go deeper in; to write more nakedly," every time he began to doubt his project. I commend him. I can't help but note that the flesh-and-blood James

Brubaker writing me, writing this book, he does the opposite—he withdraws, diverts, distracts. Maybe the other James Brubakers could learn a thing or two from Phil Elvrum. Of course, I'm complicit in this book's writing. Maybe I could learn a thing or two as well.

I can't get past the idea that Elvrum's project was *necessary* and this book is a frivolous product born out of the *real* author's privilege. Am I being too critical if I say that this project is almost selfish and will mean little to anyone outside the author? Especially when I, when *we,* don't even really know what we're talking about? Does the flesh-and-blood James Brubaker, do I, does anyone writing or narrating this book even know a single real thing about loss and grief, other than the electric discomfort that burns beneath the skin? I'm not even real. What could *I* know about discomfort? Or skin? Or grief?

If I know so little, and if this project is as unnecessary as I believe, then why don't I just stop writing? *If you really believed all this,* I imagine readers saying, *why not just walk away? Why not go start a project that's more meaningful to our historical and political contexts?* The answer, of course, is obvious: I'm not an autonomous narrator. I can't walk away from *anything.* I have been constructed, just as I am constructing, am writing the James Brubaker outside of the brackets. Does anyone believe he could walk off the page? But here's the thing: if the *real* James Brubaker made me, if he is *writing* me, then *he* is the one putting these ideas on the page. If he believes that this book is an unnecessary frivolity, why can't *he* stop writing it, or writing me to write it? I wonder: Does he not know how to stop? Is he unable to leave well enough alone? Is it a compulsion? Would anyone be surprised to discover he's a little obsessed? And so maybe all he feels like he can do, here, is soldier on and hope this story he's trying to tell starts to make sense, and hope that from this mess of interconnected scenes and narrators he will arrive at something unexpected and meaningful.]

NOTES ON THE STARMAN (19-21)

19.

Back in space, after kissing the Earth Boy, the Starman weeps and his tears undulate as they float away from his eyes. He has no idea why he kissed the human, is mortified. The Starman isn't even a sexual entity, so why did he do that? Was it just the overwhelming urge to feel close to another living being? A desire to become more human inspired by all of the different behaviors he's observed in humans over the years? The Starman doesn't know, and he is angry at himself. How can he possibly try to save the human now? He says, "I'm stupid, stupid, stupid." He says, "Why?" He says, "I ruined everything." He doesn't need to say these things, but does because he wants the Universe to hear him and keep him company so that he is not alone, even though he is still unhappy with, still doesn't trust the Universe. That is how upset the Starman is, that he would welcome companionship from the Universe.

Instead, the Starman hears a whispering buzz near his face. He sees what appears to be a small rock floating in front of him. Though he has lived long in space, encountered many things, he has never encountered anything quite like this.

The Starman says, "And what are you, little rock?"

The rock says, "sssssssssssssssssssssssssssssssssssssss."

"Can I pick you up?"

"ssssssssssssssssssssssssssssssssssss."

The Starman places the rock in his hand, closes his fingers around it. It feels heavy to him, which is strange since the Starman is in space, and there is no gravity in space. What it means for a thing to feel heavy to the Starman is that he can tell that it is dense, denser, in fact, than almost anything he has ever encountered before. He feels the rock thrum in his hand.

The rock says, "ssssssssssssssssssssssssssssssss."

The Universe says, "What do you have there, Starman?"

The Starman, even more suspicious now of the Universe for showing up at this precise moment, reluctantly opens his hand to show the rock to the Universe.

"Oh my," the Universe says. "Do you know what that is?"

The Starman shakes his head.

The Universe says, "That is part of a neutron star that must have somehow collided with another neutron star. That material in your hand is the densest matter in all of my being."

The Starman says, "It feels strange in my hand, like a writhing baby chick, like they have on Earth."

"That is no baby."

"I know. I was using a metaphor."

"You think too much about Earth and Earth things—baby chicks?"

The Starman doesn't say anything.

Finally, the Universe says, "And why do you keep encountering so many dead things—black holes and neutron stars? Are you drawn to the dead or are they drawn to you?"

The Starman hadn't thought about his encounters like that before, even though he knows full well that when stars stop being stars they become black holes or neutron stars.

"Those things aren't dead," the Starman says. "They're just different than they were."

The Universe says, "You are made of stars, and in linear time, which you foolishly choose to adhere to, those stars will eventually die, and then you will be dead, will be something different. All that will be left are these pieces that were once you as black holes, or neutron stars, or white dwarfs."

The Starman says, "That is correct."

The rock says, "ssssssssssssssssssssssssssssssss."

The Universe says, "I suppose you're right."

The Starman says, "What did he say?"

"Only that you should be grateful that you will probably someday end, because existing is boring."

The Starman says, "It's odd that I might be able to look at my future self and know that my stars die, know *how* they die, but I still can't look at my origin and know how and why I came to be. Why won't you tell me where I came from?"

The Universe laughs, says, "You're really worrying yourself over nothing. You'll get over this."

The rock says, "sssssssssssssssssssssssss."

The Unvierse says, "Exactly, little rock—out here, origins mean nothing."

The Starman doesn't believe anything that the Universe is saying, or that the rock is allegedly saying. No, the Starman thinks origins are important, and since he can't understand his origins, he has resolved to look at his ending in the hopes that maybe he can learn something of use, there.

*

20.

And so the Starman unmoors himself from the linear present to examine his own future and better understand the arc of his existence. He watches as, one after another, each of his stars flares up and goes supernova, only to become a black hole or a neutron star. He watches several of the stars that make up his form become planetary nebulae, the stars at their centers aged and weak before turning into white dwarves. He watches until he sees himself as but two remaining stars, still capable of sentient thought as the Starman, but diminished in form. He watches the Universe begin to contract, and then he is gone, before the Universe. Knowing this offers him no more insight into his existence. Having been confronted by his own anticlimactic end, the Starman slips back into linear time at the moment he left and his thoughts wander once again to the human. Even though the Starman's previous encounter with the human was embarrassing, the Starman can't stop thinking about his friend on Earth. And so the Starman goes to Earth, and he watches the human. After a while, the Starman grows bored, and decides to exit linear time, again—the Starman is getting more comfortable experiencing all of time at once—to look, one more time, for clues about the human's death, see if there's anything he missed that might help save the human's life. As the Starman watches the human, a strange sensation fills him and then he shivers. He feels as if he is being watched. He looks down at the human and sees him on a dark beach, looking through a telescope. *Is he looking at me*? the Starman wonders. The Starman looks harder and considers a plan that seems out of character, like something he shouldn't, or wouldn't, normally do. What's more, the Starman doesn't even know if the plan is possible—the Universe might so easily learn what's happening and thwart the idea before it even happens. It is a strange and risky thing. The Starman doesn't have a reason not to try it.

21.

The Starman returns to linear time, just after the moment he felt as if he'd been seen by the Earth Boy, and becomes a human again. But this time, he becomes an Earth Woman. The Starman doesn't fully understand why this is important, because he doesn't fully understand human sexuality and gender, but he understands enough to know that the human feels lonely, and seems to be attracted to women. The Starman bases his appearance on human standards of beauty—he makes teeth that are perfect and white, skin that is smooth, unblemished. He gives himself shapely legs, not too long or slender, gentle curves at the hips, slightly less gentle curves for breasts. When he is done, he worries that the shape he has made for himself doesn't look real. He pushes the proportions of his body around so that his form doesn't so much resemble an Earth model, but an Earth woman who mostly eats a sensible diet and can make it to the gym once or twice a week, but who also is busy with work, and can't work out as much as she likes, and sometimes drives through for fast food after late nights at the office, has a glass or two (or three) of wine two or three (or four) nights a week, and occasionally treats herself to ice cream.

The Starman worries about his eyes and hair last. For the eyes, he creates deep-brown irises, almost black, mysterious, he thinks. The dark hue will help to conceal the starfire inside him. He is most worried about his hair, as hair is the one thing he had difficulty creating on his previous attempts to appear human. He tries thick brown hair, short blond hair, red hair—none of it looks or feels right. And so he opts, again, to make his head bald, though he knows this is a risk. He produces for himself a lightweight white shirt with a plunging neckline and a high collar, which he pairs with a mid-length, sensible white skirt and sandals. He looks at himself in the reflection of a large piece of metallic space debris, makes minor adjustments to his appearance—soften a cheekbone, here, enlarge an earlobe there—and then descends to Earth, where he decides that he will call himself Abigail. There is no specific reason for this. He simply likes the name. Maybe as Abigail, the Starman can save the human.

The Starman arrives down the beach a bit from where the human is looking at the stars. He has never walked on sand before, and feels less certain than usual taking his first steps. As he approaches the human, the Starman walks through waves as they wash up onto the beach. It is dark, and late, and the stars and moon light his way. While he walks, he focuses his attention on understanding Abigail—he has decided she will be an adventurous woman whose travels are fulfilling, but leave her sometimes feeling lonely. Abigail, the Starman decides, will be looking for love, but not willing to settle. Abigail wants only a love that is true and real and powerful, but not because she *needs* that love in order to define herself, but because she believes life would be more fun if she had a love with whom to share her adventures. When the Starman sees the dark form of the human and his telescope down on the beach, he feels nervous.

Now, just a few dozen yards away from the human, the Starman is thinking of himself, of *herself*, as Abigail.

Abigail calls out, “Hello there.”

The human jumps, startled.

He says, “Hello?”

Abigail says, “Isn’t it late to be out on the beach all alone?”

The human says, “I might ask you the same thing.”

Abigail, now close enough that she can clearly see the human and his telescope, says, “Astronomer?”

The human says, “Amateur.”

Abigail says, “Lovely. What do you see?”

The human says, “The Milky Way. I’ve always wanted to see it, and Sagittarius A*.”

Then, Abigail says, “How lovely.”

The human volunteers more. “I’m here visiting my mom, and it’s just something that I always wanted to do—” He stops his sentence, not like he is cutting himself off, exactly, but like he wasn’t sure what the rest of the sentence was going to be.

Abigail doesn’t say anything, waiting for him to continue.

“Before,” he says. He repeats, “Before.”

“Before,” he finally continues, “I go back home where I can’t see many stars at all.”

“Is that what you were really going to say?” Abigail asks.

The human says, “Has anyone ever told you that you look like Ilia?”

Abigail says, “I do not know Ilia.”

The human says, “From the first *Star Trek* movie.”

He goes on to explain how Ilia is a member of the Enterprise crew, a Deltan, a bald woman with healing powers who is killed by a seemingly malicious spatial anomaly named V'ger. But then V'ger creates a replica of Ilia, an avatar for the anomaly, who boards the Enterprise and eventually—when the ship and its crew have journeyed to the center of V'ger's being, which turns out to be a Voyager probe launched by Earth, centuries prior—"merges" with a human character named Decker so that V'ger can become one with its "creator."

The human says, "Sorry—nerd stuff."

Abigail says, "No—it's a lovely idea."

"It's an ok movie."

Abigail moves to sit in the sand beside him. She says, "My name is Abigail."

The human tells her his name, says, "I live in London." Then he flinches, says, "What's up?"

Abigail laughs.

The human says, "Sorry, I have a thing in my head."

Abigail says, "Will you show me that movie?"

"We just met."

"I'd like to see it."

The human says, "Who are you?" He gives Abigail a hard look.

For a moment, Abigail is concerned that he has seen the starfire burning inside her. She quickly looks away.

She says, "Just a lonely girl who likes to travel."

And then she kisses him, and with the sound of the surf on the beach, and the brilliant light of the moon and the stars above, one might imagine where that kiss leads.

*

[Something is about to happen. I didn't know that it was going to happen. I'm not sure the flesh-and-blood James Brubaker writing me knew it was going to happen. It just—happened. Or is about to happen. Is happening. I'm not sure what this is going to look like. I'm not sure what my role in what's to come will be. I'm not sure it's going to be ok.]

NOTES FROM THE UNIVERSE (1-3)

1

The Universe says, “Something isn't right.”

*

2

The Universe says, "I feel ill, nauseated. I am not supposed to feel nauseated, so why do my insides grind inside of me?"

The Universe is not incorrect. The Universe is not supposed to feel sick to its stomach, is not supposed to feel like its insides are grinding inside of it. But here we are.

The Universe is also confused because it is constantly inhabiting the entirety of its existence, and does not know a moment when it feels nauseated, like its insides are grinding inside of it, has never felt anything, at any moment of its existence, except for the normal things universes are supposed to feel. The Universe searches within the entirety of its being for the cause of the illness, but finds nothing out of the ordinary.

The Universe says, "I am going to be sick."

*

3

The Universe says, "HUUUUUUUUUUUUWHAAAAA AAAAAAAAARRRRRCCCCCCCCCK," which is the sound that the Universe makes when it vomits.

The Universe can feel its insides, all those inner workings and secrets, all those strings and mysteries and dark matter and gravity, spilling into the outer, the external portions of itself, and then feels the whole mess of insides and outsides being sucked back in by the well of inertia resulting from such a large expulsion of matter, as well as from the gravity of the Universe's massive form. As they flood back in, these parts recombine in new ways.

When this process is finished, the Universe as it has known itself is different, a recombined mess of all its parts. The Universe has been turned inside out, is somehow trapped inside of itself.

The Universe says, "I am no longer what I once was. This is not right."

The Universe says, "What is to be done about this? How can I fix this?"

*

[Shit. What are we even doing, here?]

{PART FOUR

NOTES FROM THE UNIVERSE (4-5)

4

To be tampered with, to be unjustly changed, to be nullified. The Universe as it previously knew itself comes to understand that it is compressed, trapped inside of a larger version of itself. The Universe can look out of its previous consciousness to the other, bigger universe outside of it. The compressed Universe knows that the outside universe is also itself, but recombined, different, and somehow separate. For a human, this might be like if one maintained their consciousness, but their physical form were squeezed into a single molecule and then put inside a new version of them that is different in subtle, unnerving ways—also, that single molecule can see into, but has no access to the new body around it. Essentially, the old Universe has been condensed, in its entirety, into a bubble, while everything that used to be buried deep inside of it has become the new dominant universe around it. The Universe doesn't understand why its consciousness is trapped in this bubble. Does the outside universe have its own consciousness? The Universe wants help, but has no one to ask. Who can help the Universe?

The Universe contains all things, is incomparable in size and scope. How *could* anyone help it? To make matters worse, the Universe begins to believe that what remains of its former self is slightly changed as well. The Universe can't quite put its finger on what is different, but everything inside of it seems more focused, now, less cluttered. This is when the Universe realizes that it exists only in the present, and not all of time at once.

"This isn't possible," the Universe whispers to itself. "I should exist in all of time."

It isn't just possible, it is fact. The Universe is like a human now—at least in its understanding of time. What's worse, the Universe remembers almost nothing from its time before; it never had to remember anything before because all of time existed at once. That is to say, the Universe remembers enough from the time before to know that its circumstances have drastically changed, but doesn't remember many details. The Universe is not happy with its current situation. The Universe is scared.

*

5.

The Universe looks at the new universe outside of itself. The Universe vaguely remembers a being made of stars in its previous incarnation, and searches the best it can in its old contained self and the new universe outside for that being. The Universe thinks that, maybe, if it can find *something* outside in the new universe, that *something* might be able to help break it out of this cell. But the Universe can only gaze out into the new outside universe, and sees no being made of stars in that new universe, finds nothing at all, really. There are black holes and other anomalies, but they are stationary, and the Universe cannot get their attention from its bubble.

"What will I do?" the Universe cries out.

The Universe weeps.

*

LIFE...IS NOT A DREAM

I text you the day before I'm set to propose. You knew it was in the works, that we'd been looking at rings. There's no doubt she'll say yes, so I tell you that it's happening tomorrow and you better get those frequent flyer miles fired up. In your response, you ask if you can see the ring, and I tell you of course you can't. I tell you how it all feels like a dream, and you say, "Jim—life is not a dream," so I answer, "Go to sleep, Spock." It's a bit from *Star Trek V.* I haven't seen you in two years—doesn't matter though. We've gone longer. The last time we were in Dayton together was Christmas 2014. You seemed unhappy, then. Talked about feeling alone. Not long after, your father visited you in London, and you visited your mother in Costa Rica, and I was worried about you—you seemed distant for a while, less responsive to texts, less active on social media. What activity you shared was different—I'm not sure how. Like you were archiving your life to share, telling stories.

Then after that trip to Costa Rica, something changed again—snapped back, and somehow better. When I message you to see how you are, your answers are evasive but upbeat, always redirecting to ask about my work at the university, my relationship with B., my parents, our mutual friends. You've already told me you won't be able to make it to Ohio for Christmas in December—no reason given—but the minute we set a date, we should tell you so that you can arrange travel. Sometimes I feel guilty about what our friendship looks like now—me always sharing, glowing, brimming with enthusiasm over this dream of a life I'm living. I've told you, recently, how I planned to propose—at a park where we got lost as teenagers the first time we dated, how I'd take her to a clearing in the park where stone fireplaces still stand from an otherwise vanished cabin, the spot where I first told her I loved her all those years ago. You responded with only a series of emojis, the first one a blushing smiley, the next three all puking. Then you wrote, "That is the most *you* proposal possible." I've told you about Parker and the thing in her head, and Dave's art shows, and the stories I'm writing, and how my parents are doing, and how our old mutual friends' parents are doing, which I generally find out through my own parents—and all I really know about how you're doing is that you're cautiously optimistic about the news of a new *Star Trek* show, updates on occasional books you've read, and detailed accounts of your burgeoning interest in astral photography, which, you say, "changed your life." Truth is, I don't really know fuck all about what's going on with you—but you seem happy, and that's all that matters.

NOTES ON ABIGAIL (1-3)

1.

After making contact with the human, Abigail became the Starman and returned to space. There was much to attend to. Once in space, Abigail assumed another shape, this time that of the Starman taking the form of an astronaut, in the hope of not being detected by the Universe, whom she didn't want to deal with at the moment. She pulverized asteroids to dust, and from the dust recombined strands of precious metals: gold, silver, platinum. She fashioned them into exquisite necklaces and rings, which she hid on the moon until she could find ways to sell them on Earth.

When she resumed her form as Abigail and returned to Earth, she was not, at first, concerned with finding the Earth Boy. Instead, she took the necklaces and rings to a jeweler, who said, "I have no use for more trinkets from ex-husbands who were caught cheating." But after some prodding from Abigail, the jeweler looked closer, saw that the jewelry's intricate designs were unlike anything he had seen before, and offered two thousand dollars for the lot. Abigail didn't know it—how could she—but her jewelry might have fetched far more had she taken it to a more reputable dealer. It didn't matter though—two thousand dollars was enough to get an apartment, a phone. Abigail needed a phone.

The night they met, after Abigail and the human made love on the beach, after they walked back into town—him carrying his telescope, her carrying his chair, their two free hands held between them, fingers locked—and after they'd shared a breakfast of huevos rancheros and coffee at a restaurant that had just opened for the morning, the human asked Abigail for her phone number. Abigail said, "I've lost my phone, that won't help, but give me yours. I promise to call as soon as I get a new one."

In that moment, Abigail had quietly panicked—how would she build a life? How could she make this work?

The human said, "And where is home?"

Abigail said, "Minnesota."

The human said, "I'm from there. I mean originally." He took his glasses off and cleaned them with his shirt, said, "Whereabouts?"

Abigail didn't know what to say, so she said, "Up north."

"Ouch—bad winters."

"Very bad."

When they were done with breakfast, Abigail took the human's number, and kissed him on his forehead.

The human said, "I'm never going to hear from you again, am I?"

Abigail said, "You will."

*

2.

With her almost-unlimited access to asteroids and the precious metals they contain, it took Abigail only a few Earth days to establish a residence in Bemidji, Minnesota. The city is north enough to fit the lie Abigail had told, and populous enough that she could blend in.

Once settled Abigail purchased a phone and a service plan, paying in cash. It wasn't hard for her to make money. She could travel back to space to make her jewelry, then descend to any city she chose to sell it. Having built a life for herself—just enough so her apartment gave the appearance that she had lived a life on Earth: a sofa and chair, a bed, a small breakfast table, a television, a few knickknacks purchased in antique stores—Abgail phoned the human.

When he answered, Abigail said his name like a question.

The human said, "That's me. Who's calling?"

When Abigail said her name out loud, she was rewarded with a boisterous shout.

"You called!" the human said. "I didn't think you'd call, but you called!" Then, clearly away from the phone, directed elsewhere, at a coworker or friend, perhaps: "She called!"

When the human's excitement settled, he asked Abigail if she was back in Minnesota. She said she was. He asked her about the rest of her trip. She said it was fine, but that she was excited to return home so she could call him.

He said, "I'm glad you did."

She said, "When can I see you again?"

*

3.

Now, Abigail and the human are, as they say on Earth, "an item." Sometimes, still, though, when she knows the human is busy with work, Abigail takes the form of the Starman and returns to space. After several trips to collect materials for jewelry, as the Starman taking the form of an astronaut with no interference from the Universe, she no longer pretends to be anything but the Starman. She contemplates turning into a Starwoman, now, but is worried that the Universe will be suspicious of her change. Abigail can't stay for too long when she returns to space, in case her boyfriend, yes, that's what he is, now, sends her a text message or tries to call her, but she told him, up front, that she's not the kind of person who is always around her phone. She told him that she finds that lifestyle oppressive, so he shouldn't take it personally if she's slow to respond. She also told him that she doesn't believe in social media, so she doesn't have to worry about communicating with him that way. And so Abigail spends many of her days in space, mostly looking down on Earth hoping to catch a glimpse of the human through London's smog.

Sometimes Abigail contemplates what it felt like to have sex on the beach with the human—it was interesting. She liked having the human inside of her, and when she considers how humans think about sex and gender, she wonders if she's always maybe been more of a Starwoman, but never really had the frame of reference to know what that meant until now. Afterall, the Starman never had actual sex organs, no star-penis connected to star-testicles, and mainly considered himself male because, because—Abigail doesn't know why she always considered herself male, before. When she used to masturbate in space as the Starman, with genitals fabricated from stardust, she never really felt anything. This is just a thing Abigail used to do as the Starman because she was bored and she knew humans do it.

Sometimes Abigail wonders if she really actually liked the sex so much, or if in the union between bodies she felt not alone in a way she'd never felt not alone before. She wonders if maybe a lot of humans don't like sex so much, but find comfort in the union of bodies. The more she thinks about sex, the stranger it seems, and the more she thinks that this must be the case, that not all humans actually like sex. We should forgive Abigail this naïve thought, as she is *not* human, and has certainly not engaged much with Earth's popular culture, which is loaded with sex because many humans are *obsessed* with sex. Granted, there are *some* humans who aren't. Abigail doesn't really understand any of this, though.

Sometimes Abigail worries that she has tricked the human into a slow but steadily progressing romantic entanglement with a cosmic being, and that she is somehow hurting the human, or that the human will someday discover the truth of all this and Abigail will once again be alone. If nothing else, the Starman has discovered, almost immediately, that he is more comfortable as Abigail than as the Starman. Maybe this was meant to be? Maybe he was never meant to be a man at all? Surely, the Universe would not approve of this plan—but maybe the Starman was always meant to save the human. Maybe this is supposed to happen. And anyway, fuck the Universe.

Sometimes Abigail works on her appearance, careful not to change the features of her face or the shape of her body too much, but always concentrating on making hair that looks like real human hair. Through her various attempts, she produces hair that looks like an animal's fur, hair that looks like strands of pasta, hair that looks almost like human hair but smells like rotting seaweed, hair that looks like seaweed, hair that has all the properties of real human hair but that is impossibly heavy, meaning that Abigail would have to be careful not to let her hair splay out across the human's chest for fear of crushing him, hair that looks like electricity, hair that looks like the rings of Saturn, hair that looks like upholstery, and, finally, hair that looks like, smells like, feels like *hair*. Abigail is ecstatic, feels a surprising flutter and sigh inside of herself when she thinks she has gotten the hair right. On Earth, as Abigail, in Abigail's apartment, surrounded by Abigail's things, Abigail looks in the mirror in her bathroom and marvels at her long, beautiful hair. How thrilling it feels to be Abigail.

More and more, Abigail stops becoming the Starman, doesn't do anything at all but stay on Earth and practice being Abigail. She goes to the diner and eats. Even though Abigail doesn't have a digestive tract—the starfire inside her incinerates whatever food and drink she consumes—she still sometimes goes to the bathroom and sits on the toilet and pretends to expel waste from her body, just because that's what humans do. She goes to shops and browses, sometimes buying a trinket or article of clothing to take back to her apartment. She likes the feel of accumulating possessions, adding texture, in the form of glass birds and silk scarves, to the life she has created. She goes to movies, at first wondering why humans find them so enthralling when the infinite mysteries of space are just beyond their planet's atmosphere. But eventually, while watching *How to Be Single* alone at a matinee, even though the movie isn't good at all, she begins to appreciate the ways these movies show how humans feel things, how these people find important such seemingly insignificant gestures and moments. She thinks to herself that she should learn how to find seemingly insignificant things important, and before long, she begins to talk to shop clerks about the objects she has at home already while trying to buy new objects, begins to talk to her hairdresser—yes, she has a hairdresser, now—about the best ways to care for her hair, and begins to talk to everyone about the man she is seeing in London.

One woman, a barista at a coffee shop Abigail frequents, says to her one day, "That's far away—are you going to go live with him?"

Abigail, having not thought that far ahead, says, "Maybe eventually?"

And the woman says, "Living in a big city like that, a good man has a lot of options. If he's the real deal, you'd best lock him down."

"Lock him down," Abigail repeats.

*

[So we're now in the business of reinvention. I can say with authority that the Starman, though I'm not writing that section, is currently reinventing himself as Abigail, and has already reinvented the Universe. Meanwhile, the narrator outside of the brackets, the one I *am* ostensibly writing, hasn't made an appearance for many pages, since he decided that maybe the ways that he was handling his dead friend's death weren't productive, or helpful, and that maybe there was a better way through his grief. I wonder what the real James Brubaker thinks about that—on the one hand, the James Brubaker outside the brackets and I are both extensions of him, so I suppose he supports the James Brubaker outside the bracket's change of heart. But then, here we are—in a reinvented universe with a reinvented Starman. Even the other James Brubaker outside the brackets, though we've not seen him in this section yet, has been reinvented because of the Starman. As for that other narrator, we'll see him again, soon, sort of. He'll be different. Everything is different.]

NOTES ON ABIGAIL (4-5)

4.

Abigail is on one of her now-rare trips back into space as the Starman to acquire more precious metals to exchange for money. She is fashioning gold dust into fine jewelry when the Universe says, "You are a being made of stars!"

Abigail, in the form of the Starman, says, "Yes, you know that."

The Universe says, "Of course. Of course I know that." Then: "I was hoping I'd find you. Where have you been?"

Abigail notes that the Universe seems strange. She says, "On Earth."

The Universe says, "Earth. Yes, Earth. And what have you been doing on Earth?"

Abigail says, "Learning about humans."

The Universe says, "And why are you doing that?"

"Humans make me feel less alone."

"And how do they do that?"

Abigail says, "They're good to talk to. They care for one another."

"How strange."

"Something is different about you. Are you ok?"

"In fact, I'm not. I need your help with something."

Abigail asks what the Universe needs.

The Universe says, "I don't imagine you've noticed, with all the time you've been spending on Earth, that something unnerving is happening to me?"

Abigail says, "Unnerving how?"

The Universe explains about being changed and how the things inside of it spilled out and how everything that had been outside before was pulled inside, compressed into a small, flat ball. The Universe explains how its old self, everything in it, seems to be contained inside a bubble or pocket within that new universe outside.

Abigail says, "A flat ball is a circle."

The Universe says, "Not flat like two-dimensional flat, but flat in the sense that it doesn't have—" the Universe cuts itself off, says, "that's beside the point."

"What happened?"

"I don't know."

"Can I do anything to help?"

"I hope so."

"Something specific?"

"Look," the Universe says, "I don't have a clue what's happening to me. I barely remembered you existed, and then I couldn't find you and thought maybe you hadn't existed."

Abigail, relieved to be facing less scrutiny than expected, says, "I don't have any idea what I could do to help. But let me know."

The Universe says, "I will."

As the conversation ends, Abigail thinks that she's never seen the Universe so downtrodden before, so unsettled. She is surprised that the Universe, itself, doesn't know what has happened. Abigail wonders how concerned she should be. After all, she would hate to grow more attached to her boyfriend, and to humans in general, only to see them all obliterated by some strange, unexplained phenomenon taking place in this universe within a universe.

*

5.

On Earth, it is early 2016, and after several months, Abigail has not turned into the Starman and gone into space for a very long time. After the barista at the local coffee shop said the thing to Abigail about locking her man down, Abigail decided that it was time to begin pursuing a more serious relationship with him. She started messaging him regularly, several times during the day, and then video chatting with him at night. Now, on the recommendation of a magazine she read while waiting for an appointment with her hairdresser, Abigail regularly sends her lover unsolicited nudes of herself in provocative poses, which prompts him to send pictures of his erect penis in return. She responds with emojis, like a tongue sticking out of a mouth, or phrases like "yum,"—these responses, too, she learned of from the same magazine—not because she is *that* excited about seeing his erect penis, but because she wants him to know she desires him. Still, she frets that she could lose him because their relationship is long distance.

Abigail thinks about viewing all of time at once like she did a few times when she was the Starman. Perhaps, Abigail thinks, she can see what becomes of her relationship with the human. Abigail tries this, but can inhabit only her present moment. She wonders if maybe her alter ego's ability to see all of time might be hampered by her human form, and so Abigail returns to space as the Starman, assuming the alternate form as she crosses the threshold of Earth's atmosphere into space. Alas, even as the Starman, Abigail can still see only the present. Then something else strange occurs to her—when she tried looking at all of time before, she never saw herself experiencing the things she's been experiencing as Abigail. How can that be? She should have seen her relationship with the human, and seen her life as Abigail as part of that. Surely she would have known about the sex on the beach while experiencing all of time at once. Here, it occurs to Abigail that either she couldn't see her new life on Earth because she has become more Abigail than Starman, and so the Starman wasn't privy to Abigail's life and experiences, or everything that is happening now is happening outside of the timeline of the previous universe and so Abigail *couldn't* see it when she was the Starman. But how could *that* be?

For now, though, Abigail wants to try to understand what is happening to time, so she calls out to the Universe.

She says, "Universe, is time working as it's supposed to?"

The Universe says, "Is that my old friend the Starman?"

Abigail says it is, then asks about time again.

The Universe explains that it used to know all of time at once, and now it does not. Abigail nods vigorously, adding verbal cues like "mmmhmm," and "yes," and "exactly," as the Universe speaks.

Abigail says, “So it’s not just me then.”

The Universe says, “No, I believe it is all of time inside this whatever-it-is we are in. But I’m surprised you’re just noticing—this has been happening for some time.”

Abigail asks how long.

The Universe says, “I don’t know, a few months? Maybe longer? A day? Several years? I’m not accustomed to keeping track of time.” Then: “You’re seriously just noticing this?”

Abigail says, “I’ve had little use, recently, for nonlinear time.”

*

JIM, YOUR NAME IS JIM -or- TWO WEDDINGS

You come to the States in 2017 for my second wedding. We stay up late the night before. There is a party at a wine bar in St. Louis—or not a party, exactly, but a gathering, an arrival. B. and I asked friends and family to come, and so they come to talk and drink. I sip a four-ounce pour of WhistlePig and talk to parents, and aunts, and uncles, and cousins. You play pool in the next room with some of our old friends. As the crowd disperses, B. pulls you aside, tells you to make sure I get back to the hotel. Even though we own a house in St. Louis, I will stay at the wedding hotel because of superstitions, and because of pragmatism—it will be easier in the morning if I don't have to get up and get out of the house before B. can start getting ready.

Eventually, at the wine bar, it is just you and me and Parker and another old friend, an artist named Dave. We take a cab across town to another bar and we eat sandwiches. Then Parker and Dave return to their spouses at the hotel. You and I, we stay out, take another cab to a coffee shop that is open all night.

We order two decaf Americanos and sit out at a table on the sidewalk, watching drunk young professionals stagger home or into cabs. I say, "I miss caffeine," and I do, because caffeine makes me anxious, so I mostly avoid it. You say, "I still drink plenty, I just want to sleep tonight."

I say, "We're getting old." You say, "It's not so bad." I say, "I'm glad that you're here." You say, "I wouldn't have missed it for the world."

The day before, I picked you up at the airport, late in the evening. You'd found flights that brought you from London to St. Louis, but didn't arrive until almost midnight. You said you'd take a cab, but I told you that wasn't ok. How could I let you take a cab?

I sat in the airport's waiting area, rereading *Ficciones* until I caught a glimpse of your bald, shiny head and two-day stubble, the memory of a scar on your nose from when you fell before my first wedding. Though you looked the same, you seemed somehow lighter, happier. I hugged you. You said, "Jim, your name is Jim." I said, "Yes." You said, "The ship, out of danger?" I said, "You saved the ship. You saved us all. Don't you remember?"

And we both laughed, having once again, as we had many times before, successfully completed an approximation of an exchange from *Star Trek III: The Search for Spock*. Neither of us counts the film as a favorite in the franchise, but you latched on to the Jim line when we were in high school and used it to greet me ever since. Of course, in the film, the exchanges are reversed—it begins with Spock asking if the ship is out of danger, a repetition of one of his last lines before he dies in *The Wrath of Khan*, and then Kirk says, "You saved the ship, etc...," and then Spock says "Jim, your name is Jim." But it works better, for our purposes, if we start with the Jim part, and so we do, and that's what we did when you arrived in St. Louis.

But outside of the coffee shop, I tell you that you look happy, that London must be treating you well. I ask you what changed.

You say, "Not so much London." I ask what that means. You smile. I ask again. You say, "I've met someone." I say, "The fuck you have." You say, "No, really. I've been talking to her for a while." I say, "Talking to her?" Then: "Like Portia?" You tell me it isn't, that she lives in the States, but that you met her in-person first, last summer, have kept in touch, and the two of you have traveled to see each other several times since. You tell me that you applied for a transfer at work, that you'll be moving to Detroit in the spring, and once you're settled, she'll move from Minnesota to join you. "I haven't proposed yet," you say, "but we're talking."

I tell you I'm happy for you. I tell you of course this was going to happen for you, we all knew it, it was just a matter of time. I say, "And how long is *a while*?" You say, "Just over two years." I say, "Why didn't you bring her?" You say, "Your wedding is about you. We didn't want to make it about us." I tell you that is a bad reason, that you should have told me, it would have been fine. I ask, "Two years? Why haven't you told me? Have you told anyone?" You haven't, you didn't want to jinx it, and with another long distance relationship, after Portia, you didn't want to deal with the jokes, at least until you knew it was *real,* was worth sharing. I say, "That's fair."

You ramble about how much you've wanted to tell me about her, how much you wanted to tell everyone that you'd just told your own parents a few months prior, and had sworn them to secrecy. You say, "They were thrilled." I say, "You were pretty rough last time I saw you." And you had been. The last time I saw you, three years prior, you wept for how lonely you were. You say, "I met her the summer after that trip to Ohio."

You pass your phone across the table to me. The picture on the screen is a selfie of you and a beautiful woman, both smiling. Yours is an honest smile, one that I know, but haven't seen in a while. Her smile looks natural, effortless, like she has never had an easier time smiling than in the moment that picture was taken. Her eyes are stunning—they crackle with a rare energy.

I say, "I'll be damned. Tell me about her. What's her name?" You say, "I met her in Costa Rica. She was traveling. When I was there visiting Mom." You say, "Her name is Abigail."

[Is what we're doing here wrong? I'm uncomfortable with this development. This is part of the unexpected reinvention. The part of the novel that was unexpected to the flesh-and-blood James Brubaker and me. Of course, much of this novel was mapped out, its big moments, the broad strokes of its arc—but this, this, bringing our dead friend back to life through sci-fi sleight of hand, was never part of the plan. So, what changed? It became clear that the Starman and our dead friend were both lonely, both so in need of something or someone to call home. The flesh-and-blood James Brubaker writing both me and the narrator of the Starman sections didn't even see it until it was impossible to ignore—the Starman and our dead friend needed to be together, and bringing them together would bring our dead friend back to life in the text, at least for a little while, in this pocket section of the novel, set in a pocket universe. Were I the author of this book's Starman sections, I can't imagine I'd have allowed this to happen—I'm uncomfortable bringing our dead friend back to life, writing him as if he never died—but the real James Brubaker forced my hand through the Starman's actions. I suspect the flesh-and-blood James Brubaker would assert that it was the demands of the narrative that led to this development, that he uncovered the true arc of the story through the process of invention. My suspicion is that his true motives were more selfish—it's not like the union of Abigail and our dead friend was entirely organic. There are obvious questions here, after all: Why would the Starman's coming to live on Earth unravel space-time and create a pocket universe? And, on a more human level, how does Abigail's appearance in our dead friend's life make him not dead in this part of the text? Does this imply that our dead friend in the previous universe killed himself because he was lonely? Or just that Abigail's appearance in his life resulted in him making different decisions that led to him not dying? I'm not sure there's an answer for that. There should be, and I should know it. But there isn't, or if there is, I don't.]

That was October, when you came to our wedding. The following April, you message me a picture of you and Abigail, your cheeks mashed together, her hand on the side of your face, both of you sporting the same smiles as in that previous picture you showed me. It takes a moment to notice the ring on Abigail's finger. Of course there is a ring. I type back, "Holy shit!" You write, "The wedding is in August. You're going to be an usher."

B. and I drive out to Detroit early to help prepare. The ceremony is simple, small and lovely, held in the backyard of the house you bought a few months prior. The morning of the wedding, we set up forty folding chairs. An hour before, we light torches along the grassy aisle. The guest list consists of a few friends from high school, a few work friends from London and Detroit, parents, siblings, and assorted relatives. Abigail doesn't have any family in attendance. You tell me both her parents are dead. I ask, "Any other family?" You say, "Her family was small, she was an only child. Same with her parents." I say, "Shit."

After the ceremony, you pour scotch for anyone who wants it, and champagne for those who don't. Your father makes a toast, sweet and loving. The kind of toast fathers are supposed to give—cliché but sincere, he closes it with, "I'm proud of you, son, and happy to welcome Abigail into our family." Then your friend Brian makes a toast, the kind of toast friends give, a little bit of a roast, but mostly sweet, gets a good laugh by thanking Abigail for saving us from a lifetime of *your* despair. And then I give a toast. It's not anything special, a few words about how lucky I am to call you a friend, how happy I am for you to have found a love so strong, etc... etc.... Of course I close with a Trek quote, one from "The Inner Light," one of your favorite episodes of *The Next Generation*: "Live now; make now always the most precious time. Now will never come again." I'm not sure why I'm nervous, but my voice wavers. B. squeezes my hand.

After we toast and drink, Abigail approaches me and B. She says, "That was a lovely toast." I raise my glass and say, "For a lovely couple." She says, "I just watched that episode at my—" she pauses, puts joyful emphasis on the following word—"*husband's* recommendation." She hugs me. She feels astonishingly warm. She whispers, "Thank you for taking care of him all those years." I say, "I didn't, really." Then I ask, "Are you feeling ok? You feel warm." She says, "Just the August heat and nerves."

The night before the wedding, you, Parker, Brian, and I sat around the firepit in your backyard, drinking rye and smoking cigars. Being parents, both, and less accustomed to late nights, Parker and Brian turned in early, her to a guestroom with her husband, and him on the living room sofa. When it was just you and me at the firepit, I said something banal and easy, like, "I'm so happy for you." You said, "I am too." Then: "And relieved." I said, "I get that." You said, "Do you?"

I asked what you meant by that and stared into the fire waiting for a response, watched the flame's tongues whip the humid August air and spit smoke into the sky. Finally, after what felt like an hour, you said, "Remember how I used to say the Captain Kirk thing, about how I knew I'd die alone?" I said I did. You paused, took a sip of whiskey, said, "I'd never felt more alone than I did after Susan left." You said, "I was drinking. A lot. I stopped running. I was smoking two packs a day."

You told me that you'd get home from work, eat fast food, drink, play games on your computer until nine or ten, then jerk off to porn and fall asleep, probably still drinking, hopefully not smoking. You told me that all of your friends at work were having kids, and most of your friends back in the States, too. You said, "And you were going through the divorce, and then you had something new with an old love." You told me that our getting back together was hard for you, not because you weren't happy for us or didn't approve, but because it felt like it was preordained, that it was fate—to see two people who shaped each other so long ago find each other again. You were wondering when that would happen for you. I said, "Preordination is horseshit." You said, "Sure, the point is—I wasn't even sure what I was doing anymore. I don't know—"

You stopped abruptly and looked up at the sky. You said, "I never see the Starman, anymore." You added, "Sometimes I feel like I barely remember him at all." I said, "Who has time for starmen?" You said, "The last time I saw him was on the beach, the night that I met Abigail. When I met her, I told her I was out looking at the Milky Way, at Sagittarius

A*, and I was, but I was also looking for the Starman. And I saw him that night. And it was like he saw me too, and then he was gone." I said, "Maybe he brought you two together. Maybe that's what he was there for." Then: "I'm still here." I raised my glass and said, "You're still here."

The clink of our glasses sang above the fire's crackle. We finished our whiskey in silence and then I found my way to B.'s side in a hideaway bed in your home office, and you made your way back to bed beside your soon-to-be bride.

[Just to be clear, lest we assume a happy ending for all, here—and I offer this not to spoil what's to come, but as an act of kindness, so that readers might prepare themselves for the inevitable pending cruelty—our no-longer-dead-in-the-text-but-dead-in-real-life friend is going to die, and Abigail will once again be alone. This *will* happen. I'm not necessarily saying that our no-longer-dead-in-the-text-but-dead-in-real-life friend is going to die an untimely or mysterious death like he did in real life, though I suspect he will, but he is a mortal being in this text, and Abigail, while technically also mortal, will exist for millennia after our no-longer-dead-in-the-text-but-dead-in-real-life friend dies in the text. Abigail will once again be alone. That's how it has to be.]

CHRISTMAS EVE AT DENNY'S, 2018

Before long, just months after your wedding, we are in Dayton for Christmas—all of us. You and Abigail and B. and me. We spend the days with our respective families, then meet up most nights and go out on the town to see other old friends or have drinks. One night the four of us go to a holiday party at Dave and Sarah's, a less boozy affair than in past years now that most of the attendees have kids—meaning that, even though many left their kids at home with sitters, the party won't run as late as it used to. Still, it's a good party. Dave is an artist, makes these unbelievably detailed ink drawings, way back used to create beautiful, intricate works of art on the insides of matchbox covers, and he's a passionate storyteller, infinitely interesting. Sarah likes to plan and get shit done, used to act before I knew her, is good-natured as hell. So of course it's a great party even though most everyone has to be home by ten. Early in the evening, you step outside for a smoke and invite me along. I join, not just for old time's sake, but because I still enjoy smoking and take the chance to do it when I have an excuse.

Outside, you say, “Man, these kids. Seems fun.” I ask, “Getting the dad itch?” You say, “Something like that.” I ask if Abigail is on board. You don’t know. “Maybe,” you say, “she’s evasive.” Then you add, “You?” I say, “Me what?” You say, “Kids.” I say, “No,” then again, “No.” You say, “I don’t know what’s next without kids.” I don’t say anything for a moment. Then I say, “There’s always something next.” You say, “I guess so,” but not like you really mean it. You repeat, “I guess so.”

When we make our way back into the party, Dave and Sarah’s two boys, aged seven and four, are performing some kind of pageant, the older standing in the middle of the room holding an electric candle and singing the drumrolls from “The Little Drummer Boy,” while the younger runs circles around him trailing gold and silver streamers behind, shouting the chorus from “Joy to the World.” Dave is beaming, his face saying *look at my weird goddamn kids.* B. is laughing, enjoying the spectacle of someone else’s kids, knowing that she and I won’t have to get up in the middle of the night because one of them can’t sleep, or had a bad dream, or threw up. Abigail is reading, or pretending to read, something on her phone. Or maybe she’s looking at Instagram, scrolling rapidly, trying to look anywhere but at you or the children.

I turn to you, say, “Artists’ kids, man.”

You don’t seem to hear me, your face full of the promise that someday, soon, something like this could be yours.

The next night, you and I go to Parker’s. We go late. We always go late when we go to Parker’s. She and her husband, Cale, have always been night people. They’ll put their kid to bed at eight, then do whatever it is that married couples with kids do after they put their kids down at eight. That night, they told us to come over after nine.

B. is tired and has some work to finish up, and Abigail is spending time with your stepmom, so it's just you and me. I pick you up at eight, so we have time to grab some good whiskey before the stores close. Earlier, Cale sent a message, presumably unbeknownst to Parker, indicating that a celebration was in order. So we stop at the store and pick up a bottle of Kilchoman Machir Bay, nothing too fancy, but it's the scotch I bought for a toast before my and B.'s wedding, and Parker seemed to like it then, so it seems like a good pick. Because it is December and the New Year is fast approaching, the liquor store is stocked with frivolous party favors—noisemakers, cardboard hats, glasses with frames shaped to look like 2019. I pay for the scotch, and you buy a bag full of party junk, including plastic mustaches attached to sticks that we can hold over our faces to pretend we have mustaches, even though I have a full beard, and you kind of do, too—a five-day growth, we'll say. You also buy a bottle of cheap sparkling wine that you refer to as champagne, even though it isn't.

We arrive at Parker's house just after nine, sporting hats and 2019 glasses, and holding fake mustaches over our real mustaches.

When Parker opens the door, we whisper, "Happy Celebration," our agreed-upon generic greeting since we don't know what we are celebrating. Cale greets us with hugs when we enter, all of us trying to be quiet so as to not wake the kid. You say, "What's the occasion?" I pretend to blow on a noisemaker, use my finger to unroll the paper. Parker says, "My surgery is scheduled for next week, on the second." I say, "Surgery?" She says, "Come on in, I'll tell you about it."

Over scotch, Parker tells us that the prognosis is good, but not great—but not *bad*. The surgeon will cut into her head and remove the growth. There don't appear to be any particularly troubling entanglements, but the procedure, like any procedure in which a surgeon cuts into someone's brain, will be somewhat risky.

In the middle of Parker's explanation, you twitch, say, "What's up?"

It's the first time I've seen you do that on this visit, and it surprises me. At first, I'm not sure what you're doing, like I'd almost forgotten you sometimes twitch and say, "What's up?"

We all laugh. And then Parker finishes explaining that she'll need some time to recuperate. Cale says, "We're quite relieved." And you hold up a glass and say, "To getting that thing out of your head, for good." And we drink, and we laugh. And a week later Parker goes into surgery and everything is fine.

Later that night, as I drive you home to your dad's house, you say, "Do you ever get the feeling that everything is too good?" I say, "All the time, these days." You say, "We're lucky, all of us." I say, "We are." You say, "I mean, everything seems too impossibly good." I say, "Don't overthink it." You say, "I know," then: "I know." I say, "Bad shit is the exception." You say, "I keep expecting the bubble to burst." I say, "You always expect, *have always expected*, the bubble to burst." You say, "Bubbles burst." I say, "Not always." You say, "Bubbles always burst." I say, "Hopefully this bubble won't burst until you've lived a long, happy life." You tell me you don't think that Abigail wants kids. I ask why you think that. You say, "Last night, after the party, I brought it up. She didn't say much." I say, "You two just got married. Give it some time." You say, "We're not getting any younger." I say, "You've got to get out of your head, man. You're doing that thing." "That thing," you repeat. "I do that." I say, "You sure do."

* * *

On Christmas Eve, we meet at Denny's, late. We've done this almost every year for fifteen years or so. I don't remember how it started, but it was a thing for a while, a big thing, where all of us, anyone we considered a friend, would muscle through whatever family affairs we had to tend to on Christmas Eve, trickle up to Denny's one by one, and smoke and drink coffee and eat grilled cheese sandwiches or breakfast food and play euchre. Each year we were joined by various friends, a rotating array of restless twenty- and then thirty-somethings looking for an escape from more traditional holiday festivities. More recently, Christmas Eves at Denny's have just been you and me, if that, as we've missed several years due to conflicting travel schedules. That's how life goes—our friends had kids. Christmas Eve at Denny's has been replaced for them by building playsets and assembling tricycles, taking two bites out of a cookie and drinking half a glass of milk, throwing away the carrots left for the reindeer, but making sure they're wrapped in a paper towel and buried deep in the trash can. I get it.

I order a grilled cheese, no tomato, and a decaf. You order the two-egg breakfast, eggs over hard, and with sausage. When your food arrives, you scramble the eggs and hash browns together, then cut the sausage links into twelve small pieces, arrange them around the edge of the plate. You've done this for as long as we've been going to Denny's. You call your arranged plate "The Clock." Tonight, when I stare into The Clock, I see infinity. I say, "I'll miss this when you and Abigail have a kid." You say, "I won't not show up to Christmas Eve at Denny's." I say, "You will, and it will be fine." You say, "How will I celebrate my birthday?" I say, "Oh shit—I forgot." You laugh, say, "You always forget." I say, "Your food's on me."

The last time we had Christmas Eve at Denny's was three or four years ago right after Susan, when you weren't in a good place. That year, too, I forgot it was your birthday at midnight and, again, bought your food. Finally, you say, "You really don't want kids?" I say, "You know, between mid-October and the end of December—" I trail off. "No, not really," I add after a beat. "You two will change your minds," you say, waving around a piece of sausage stuck to the end of your fork. "No, we won't—I mean, maybe if we could rent one for the holidays," I say. You laugh. I say, "You seem suddenly more optimistic about your odds." You say, "Abigail can't have kids." You add, "But, she wants to adopt." I say, "She didn't tell you before you were married?" You say, "We didn't talk about kids. It didn't seem to matter." I say, "You ok with that?" You say, "Pop will be bummed that the family genes will end with me, but I don't mind." I say, "That's great." Then: "Fuck genes."

We toast with our coffee mugs.

Then it is midnight.

I wish you a happy birthday.

[The *real* James Brubaker wants me to say, on the record—Christmas Eve at Denny's was real. And our dead friend's birthday was really on Christmas Day. That's not a stupid, shitty thing built into the story to reference Christ and the resurrection since we've resurrected our friend, here in this novel. We'll call it a ham-fisted coincidence. Otherwise, I'm troubled to realize we've written ourselves into a corner where we're going to have to imagine our dead friend's child and what our dead friend is like as a father. I'm not sure why the *real* James Brubaker has decided to put us through that. I know for a fact that the *real* James Brubaker has been avoiding having me write too many scenes with our dead friend and Abigail together. I'm not sure he knows what that would look like. I suspect we're going to find out before long.]

...

No, that wasn't good enough. Let's try this: it's true that I frequently forgot that your birthday was Christmas Day. I remembered some years, but forgot others. I don't forget anymore. Usually, by the time midnight rolls around on Christmas Eve, B. and I are playing cards with my parents. Maybe we're just wrapping up. I'll look at the clock and see it's almost midnight and I'll have to choke back some tears, grit my teeth, whatever, to not let them know that, while I want to be there, fully present with them, I wish I were at Denny's with you. I just wanted to say that—because even though this novel grew out of real heartache, the majority of its contents are fiction. I like knowing there are a few true things in here. Things that no constructed narrator could possibly convey. I wanted to say this for myself

...

[What was that?]

On Christmas Day, after the family celebrations are finished, you and Abigail come to my parents' house for drinks and dessert. Due to an unseasonably warm string of days, we sit comfortably around the firepit on the back porch. You and me and Abigail sip rye I brought from my favorite distillery in St. Louis. B. drinks a vodka soda.

When the conversation reaches a lull, B. says, "So Abigail, how are you liking Detroit?" Abigail says, "It's so small." I say, "I remember once thinking it was so big." Abigail says, "You've spent time there?" I say, "Not really." Then: "Just used to go there to see bands play, back when I was in college." Abigail says, "I'm used to bigger places." B. asks, "Like London?" She adds, "I'm sure you visited." Abigail pauses, looks at her rye. "Like London," she says. B. asks, "Are you working?" Abigail tells us that she is still looking for work, has been volunteering at a small art gallery on Woodward. You say, "We don't really need the extra income." Abigail says, "We should be saving more." And you say, "Childcare will cost more than a job—but it's up to you."

B. looks at Abigail's drink, then shoots me a look. I can feel the question in her eyes, *Is she?* I say, "I didn't tell B. about your news." So you tell us about how you're planning to adopt, that you will begin the paperwork after the New Year, that you know it can take time, but that you are excited. Abigail holds your hand while you speak. You both smile. "Maybe we can get one that's housebroken," you say. We all laugh and then fall into another lull. Then, you start telling us about the stars. You show us Gemini, Taurus, Lepus, Aries. You show us Triangulum, and then Leo.

B. says, "I'm impressed." Then, with a hint of disgust in her voice: "Space." You say, "You don't like space?" Then, to me: "You married a woman who doesn't like space?" B. says, "It's infinite—it's terrifying." Abigail says, "It's not really infinite." Then: "It was his love of the stars that brought us together." Neither of you recount the story about the two of you meeting on the beach because B. and I already know it. You say, "Did I ever tell you about the Starman?" Abigail leans forward, crosses her hands on her knees. I say, "The Starman." Then: "I think I remember that." You say, "I feel like I used to see the Starman all the time. Used to keep tabs on him. But now, those memories—sometimes it's like there was never a starman at all." Abigail says, "The Starman. What is this?"

And so you tell her about how you have vague memories of watching a man made of stars in the night sky. How you weren't sure if you ever thought it was real, but you'd look up some nights, and there he would be, moving through the cosmos, doing whatever the fuck a starman does. Abigail says, "You saw this Starman?" You say, "I'm not sure anymore." Then you ask me, "Did you tell me you saw him once?" I say, "Of course I saw him. How could you forget the Starman?" You say, "I feel like he used to be important to me."

I lift my glass, say, "Let our bodies fail before our memories." B. says, "Easy there, old man." You raise your glass and the two of us sip our rye. You say, "That's not it though. This is different." Abigail says, "What do you remember?" You say, "I don't know." You look up at the sky. Abigail looks up at the sky. We all look up at the sky. You say, "Not much at all." Abigail says, "Maybe it'll come to you." I say, "Maybe a little more rye will knock some memories loose." I catch your face in the fire's light and am surprised at the intensity of your expression—you look terrified. You say, "I don't think there's anything to knock loose." Abigail says, "There's got to be something." You say, "It's not a big deal, it's fine. Just a young man's flight of fancy." Abigail says, "I'd like to know about it. If it was important to you." You say, "I guess if it were important to me, I'd remember. Maybe someday it will come back to me. Maybe when I'm least expecting it."

Abigail shifts back in her seat and is mostly quiet for the rest of the evening. None of us say much, really. I can sense your unease. Of course there was a Starman. You used to talk about him all the time. I don't push, though. There's no sense untangling whatever it is any of us feel when confronted with the fragility of memory and the weight of mortality. Was there a Starman? Did you and I once talk about the Starman? I can't remember, and so I sit silent, haunted by the fragility of memory and the weight of my, of our, mortality. Maybe bad shit *is* always right around the corner. Maybe bubbles always *do* burst. And maybe neither of those things matters because nothing about anything we do matters.

I say, "I'm going to get the birthday boy another drink," grab your glass, and head inside—a small act to stave off the very familiar, very real dread settling over me.

...

Here's something else that maybe the narrator in the brackets doesn't know: that dread is real, too. I don't understand it. Some mornings I wake up and am filled with it. Is that normal? Do people with nine-to-five jobs and kids feel that dread? Did you feel that dread? The real you, not this fantasy version of you. Do those people with "normal" lives, with kids and office jobs, dread the emptiness of their existence and the way it one day all just stops and we become nothing? Maybe they're too busy. Or maybe they drown it in religion. Or maybe that dread is a hardwired part of the drive to procreate—whatever. All I know is that when I feel that dread, that acute sensation of feeling powerless, of being so small, adrift in the cosmos, not a part of anything tangible, exactly—I'm just a thing inside of, loosely affiliated with, a much, much bigger thing. I know, from my own experience, that feeling powerless is hard, especially for those used to privilege, used to everyone and everything in the world making way for their success, telling them how great they are. And so when we are confronted with the truth of our existence, the realization that we truly are powerless to the whims of the universe, we don't know how to react. We lash out, we get mad, we get drunk, we get high, we break down, we lose our minds, we break shit, we hurt people. Maybe this novel is my version of that. Or maybe it's my attempt to move beyond that. Because, though feeling powerless and the accompanying dread have long been a part of my life—not daily, but sometimes—I'd never felt the dread of powerlessness so much as when I learned you had died. I'd never felt as powerless as I did when I realized I'd never know how or why you died. I'd never felt as powerless as I did when I knew I'd never get to say goodbye. The narrator in the brackets couldn't know this, or say this, so I will: This section of this novel set in a pocket universe—this is the extent of my power. This section of this novel is me imposing my will on your life, or your death, perhaps, by making you not dead. Is me imposing my will on the universe, saying—*this is how the universe should fucking be.* I'm writing this section for me. I am selfish. Acknowledging this doesn't make it any less self-indulgent or unhealthy. Doesn't make it any less selfish.

That's enough from me, though—where's the narrator in the brackets? I created him for a reason

...

[That was unexpected, to say the least. In response to the question of one's inability to accept powerlessness in the face of an uncaring universe, as discussed in that last bit by my creator, it would seem, I would like to offer to him a brief quote from a "A New Refutation of Time," an essay by his favorite author, Jorge Luis Borges. Over the course of the essay, Borges argues first that time is comprised of a series of discrete moments, that "each moment we live exists, not the imaginary sum of those moments." But Borges ultimately goes on to argue, after interjecting "*And yet, and yet...*," that "temporal succession," that *destiny*, itself, is real, is "irreversible and iron-bound," before finally arriving at the conclusion that: "time is the substance of which I am made. Time is a river that sweeps me along, but I am the river; it is a tiger that mangles me, but I am the tiger; it is a fire that consumes me, but I am the fire." Finally, he writes, "The world, unfortunately, is real; I, unfortunately, am Borges." Yes, I now see in the real James Brubaker's writing of this book the same begrudging acceptance of that reality, unfortunately, unfortunately. I wonder, is it enough for him to say, for *us* to say, "The world, unfortunately, is real; we, unfortunately, are Brubaker"? *And yet, and yet...*I am still here, stuck in these brackets.]

NOTES ON ABIGAIL (6)

6.

Abigail has been busy—the Earth Boy fell in love with her, he proposed to her, they got married, and now she lives with him in Detroit, Michigan. Abigail is happy. She is also worried. Tonight, Christmas night, in Ohio, at her father-in-law's house, she can't sleep. Even though Abigail is Abigail, now, she used to be the Starman, and she knows all of the things that the Starman knew, and so she is perplexed, first, because she has recently learned that her husband used to be able to see the Starman, and second, because memories of the Starman's existence and anything having to do with said existence seem to be fading from his consciousness. Abigail wonders if these developments on Earth have anything to do with the Universe's current conundrum. Abigail hopes the two aren't related, but an uneasy feeling nagging at her stomach—as the stars inside her churn in a way that might be analogous to human nausea—tells her that they are.

Abigail worries that she, herself, might be fading from existence. But how can that be? What could make Abigail, who was once the mighty Starman, disappear as if she'd never *been* at all?

While Abigail's husband sleeps beside her, the only sound in the room is the ticking of an old wall clock.

Abigail wants to test the integrity of her human body, and the starfire locked tightly inside. First, she goes to the bathroom and uses a pair of tweezers to pinch her skin. The pinch stings. Next, careful to be quiet so as not to wake anyone, she goes to the kitchen, takes a knife, and runs it gently along the edge of her finger, not to cut herself, but to see how her skin responds to the coolness of the blade's edge. It feels like a blade's edge on her skin. Finally, Abigail takes a spoon from the silverware drawer, opens her mouth, tilts back her head, and drops the spoon straight down her throat. The spoon is incinerated in a fraction of a second—her starfire is as strong as ever. Having found no sign of degradation, no sign that she is weakening or fading from existence, Abigail explores other possibilities.

Perhaps the easiest explanation, Abigail supposes, is that human memory is much more frail than she realized—her husband is simply starting to forget being enamored with the Starman. Similarly feasible, Abigail's husband isn't so much forgetting the Starman as he is repressing memories that he might find odd or embarrassing now that he's a more mature adult. But neither of these options rings true. Perhaps there is a simpler explanation—maybe the thing in Abigail's husband's head, the thing that she put there years ago, in linear Earth-time, when she was the Starman, is causing the memory loss. Granted, doctors haven't connected the thing in his head to any of his higher brain functions, including his memory.

What will happen if Abigail is completely forgotten? This thought is too frightening for her. So, instead she contemplates the nature of time paradoxes. She thinks about how she used to think of her husband as the Earth Boy and wonders if, maybe, he, *the Earth Boy*, was intended to know the Starman, but now that he is older and has become Abigail's husband is meant to know only Abigail, and so memories of the Starman are being replaced by Abigail. Abigail likes this idea. Could it all be so simple? The Starman is slowly fading from existence because she has become Abigail? Abigail wonders, too, if the thing in her husband's head is even still there—it was put there by the Starman, after all, not Abigail. He still occasionally will twitch and say, "What's up," but not as often as he used to. Is that because the thing in his head is fading? Or maybe it's gone entirely and the twitch and "what's up" is just a habit, now, a nervous tic. In a matter of moments, Abigail has shifted from the terror of thinking something terrible was happening to her, to feeling a sense of peace at accepting the unknowing, accepting her circumstances. If the Starman is fading from existence, she concludes, so be it. I am Abigail now, and Abigail, clearly, is not fading from existence. Abigail closes her eyes and slowly falls asleep.

*

[I want to hear from the *real* James Brubaker again. Where is he? I want to read what he has to say about Abigail, about the way she has found happiness. When he made an appearance earlier, he discussed the tension between his privilege and how, because of that privilege, the death of his dead friend came to feel insurmountable—an event he cannot change or undo created a situation in which he couldn't possibly get his way. And so in writing this novel, he found a way to reimagine the universe so he *could* get his way, even if only on the page. To an extent, then, he is not unlike the Starman, who, admittedly without knowing what he was doing, seems to have reshaped the whole of the Universe to get his way and not feel so lonely, at least for a little while. Abigail, on the other hand, has found happiness through embracing her powerlessness. Rather than raging against her present fragility, she gives herself over to it, accepts it. I want to hear the *real* James Brubaker speak to Abigail's vulnerability, her acceptance, how she has let go of her old self and become new. I'm sure he must realize the important lesson, there, right? I know that this type of acceptance isn't easy, but...]

NOTES FROM THE UNIVERSE (6-9)

6.

These days, the Universe mostly drifts in and out of sleep. Linear time is a drag. What else can the Universe really do when its entire consciousness has gone from being practically infinite to being able to experience only a tiny sliver of that infinity, and in sequential order? Sometimes, the Universe finds a modicum of pleasure in the hazy space between sleep and wakefulness. Truthfully, it's the sleeping part that the Universe loves so—when would the Universe, in its previous incarnation, have even had time to *think* about sleeping, what with all of time to keep it busy? Sometimes, though, in the moments before falling asleep, thoughts and images from before, from the old universe, wriggle their way into the Universe's consciousness, where it rolls those memories around in its thoughts—like a hard candy in a grandfather's mouth—savoring them before finally succumbing to sleep, and letting go, sometimes never to be retrieved. It is during one of these hypnogogic trances on the verge of sleep that the Universe remembers something important, something that explains the conundrum in which it now finds itself—something about the man made of stars, *the Starman*, and about his origin. Before the Universe can act on the memory, or even find a way to prevent it from slipping away, sleep arrives and the memory evaporates.

*

7.

When the Universe awakens, it recalls remembering something before falling asleep, but isn't sure what the something was. That is, the Universe has *no* idea what it is trying to remember. Keep in mind, the Universe doesn't even really understand the concept of *memory* because, until recently, it always existed in all moments of time at once. But the Universe needs to remember, now, because it suspects that the thing it has forgotten might help it figure out how to undo this unusual situation in which it has found itself. The Universe ties a string around its finger, hoping to retroactively coax the memory out of hiding. The Universe tries retracing its steps, tries thinking about something else entirely to lure the memory back, tries taking a nap to see if, upon waking, the thing it is trying to remember will return. None of this works, not exactly. As it happens, though, in the course of trying, the Universe encounters a ghost black hole. How strange, the Universe thinks, to encounter a ghost black hole inside a *pocket* universe. The Universe decides that this could be quite advantageous.

The Universe says, “Is it strange to be a ghost of a black hole from a previous universe inside this universe that is really just a pocket universe?”

The Ghost Black Hole says, “WOOOOOoooooOooOoo OooOooOOOOOOOWWWWOO.”

“I can see how it might not seem that different to you.”

“WOooooooOOOoooooooooooooOOOwwwWwwoow-wOOWOWOowowWOOOOOOOOO.”

The Universe leans in, says, “You don’t say.”

“ooooOOOooo.”

“Yes, I have noticed that something is amiss.”

“oooooooooooooooooooooooo?”

The Universe says, “Well, what do *you* think is causing it?”

The Ghost Black Hole says, “ØØØØØØØØØØØØØØØØ ØØØØØØØØØØØØØØØØØØØØØØØØØØØØØØØØØ ØØØØØØØØØØØØØØØØØØØØØØØØØØØØØØØØØ ØØØØØØØØØØØØØØØØØØØØØØØØØØØØØØØØØ ØØØØØØØØØØØØØØØØØØØØØØØØØØØØØØØØØ ØØØØØØØØØØØØØØØØØØØØØØØØØØØØØØØØØ ØØØØØØØØØØØØØØØØØØØØØØØØØØØØØØØØØ ØØØØØØØØØØØØØØØØØØØØØØØØØØØØØØØØØ ØØØØØØØØØØØØØØØØØØØØØØØØØØØØØØØØØ ØØØØØØØØØØØØØØØØØØØØØØØØØØØØØØØØØ ØØØØØØØØØØØØØØØØØØØØØØØØØØØØØØØØØ ØØØØØØØØØØØØØØØØØØØØØØØØØØØØØØØØØ ØØØØØØØØØØØØØØØØØØØØØØØØØØØØØØØØØ ØØØØØØØØØØØØØØØØØØØØØØØØØØØØØØØØØ ØØØØØØØØØØØØØØØØØØØØØØØØØØØØØØØØØ ØØØØØØØØØØØØØØØØØØØØØØØØØØØØØØØØØ ØØØØØØØØØØØØØØØØØØØØØØØØØØØØØØØØØ ØØØØØØØØØØØØØØØØØØØØØØØØØØØØØØØØØ ØØØØØØØØØØØØØØØØØØØØØØØØØØØØØØØØØ

ØØØØØØØØØØØØØØØØØØØØØØØØØØØØØØØØ
ØØØØØØØØØØØØØØØØØØØØØØØØØØØØØØØØ
ØØØØØØØØØØØØØØØØØØØØØØØØØØØØØØØØ
ØØØØØØØØØØØØØØØØØØØØØØØØØØØØØØØØ
ØØØØØØØØØØØØØØØØØØØØØØØØØØØØØØØØ
ØØØØØØØØØØØØØØØØØØØØØØØØØØØØØØØØ
ØØØØØØØØØØØØØØØØØØØØØØØØØØØØØØØØ
ØØØØØØØØØØØØØØØØØØØØØØØØØØØØØØØØ
ØØØØØØØØØØØØØØØØØØØØØØØØØØØØØØØØ
ØØØØØØØØØØØØØØØØØØØØØØØØØØØØØØØØ
ØØØØØØØØØØØØØØØØØØØØØØØØØØØØØØØØ
ØØØØØØØØØØØØØØØØØØØØØØØØØØØØØØØØ
ØØØØØØØØØØØØØØØØØØØØØØØØØØØØØØØØ
ØØØØØØØØØØØØØØØØØØØØØØØØØØØØØØØØ
ØØØØØØØØØØØØØØØØØØØØØØØØØØØØØØØØ
ØØØØØØØØØØØØØØØØØØØØØØØØØØØØØØØØ
ØØØØØØØØØØØØØØØØØØØØØØØØØØØØØØØØ
ØØØØØØØØØØØØØØØØØØØØØØØØØØØØØØØØ
ØØØØØØØØØØØØØØØØØØØØØØØØØØØØØØØØ
ØØØØØØØØØØØØØØØØØØØØØØØØØØØØØØØØ
ØØØØØØØØØØØØØØØØØØØØØØØØØØØØØØØØ
ØØØØØØØØØØØØØØØØØØØØØØØØØØØØØØØØ
ØØØØØØØØØØØØØØØØØØØØØØØØØØØØØØØØ
ØØØØØØØØØØØØØØØØØØØØØØØØØØØØØØØØ
ØØØØØØØØØØØØØØØØØØØØØØØØØØØØØØØØ
ØØØØØØØØØØØØØØØØØØØØØØØØØØØØØØØØ
ØØØØØØØØØØØØØØØØØØØØØØØØØØØØØØØØ
ØØØØØØØØØØØØØØØØØØØØØØØØØØØØØØØØ
ØØØØØØØØØØØØØØØØØØØØØØØØØØØØØØØØ
ØØØØØØØØØØØØØØØØØØØØØØØØØØØØØØØØ
ØØØØØØØØØØØØØØØØØØØØØØØØØØØØØØØØ
ØØØØØØØØØØØØØØØØØØØØØØØØØØØØØØØØ

ØØØØØØØØØØØØØØØØØØØØØØØØØØØØØØØØ
ØØØØØØØØØØØØØØØØØØØØØØØØØØØØØØØØ
ØØØØØØØØØØØØØØØØØØØØØØØØØØØØØØØØ
ØØØØØØØØØØØØØØØØØØØØØØØØØØØØØØØØ
ØØØØØØØØØØØØØØØØØØØØØØØØØØØØØØØØ
ØØØØØØØØØØØØØØØØØØØØØØØØØØØØØØØØ
ØØØØØØØØØØØØØØØØØØØØØØØØØØØØØØØØ
ØØØØØØØØØØØØØØØØØØØØØØØØØØØØØØØØ
ØØØØØØØØØØØØØØØØØØØØØØØØØØØØØØØØ
ØØØØØØØØØØØØØØØØØØØØØØØØØØØØØØØØ
ØØØØØØØØØØØØØØØØØØØØØØØØØØØØØØØØ
ØØØØØØØØØØØØØØØØØØØØØØØØØØØØØØØØ
ØØØØØØØØØØØØØØØØØØØØØØØØØØØØØØØØ
ØØØØØØØØØØØØØØØØØØØØØØØØØØØØØØØØ
ØØØØØØØØØØØØØØØØØØØØØØØØØØØØØØØØ
ØØØØØØØØØØØØØØØØØØØØØØØØØØØØØØØØ
ØØØØØØØØØØØØØØØØØØØØØØØØØØØØØØØØ
ØØØØØØØØØØØØØØØØØØØØØØØØØØØØØØØØ
ØØØØØØØØØØØØØØØØØØØØØØØØØØØØØØØØ
ØØØØØØØØØØØØØØØØØØØØØØØØØØØØØØØØ
ØØØØØØØØØØØØØØØØØØØØØØØØØØØØØØØØ
ØØØØØØØØØØØØØØØØØØØØØØØØØØØØØØØØ
ØØØØØØØØØØØØØØØØØØØØØØØØØØØØØØØØ
ØØØØØØØØØØØØØØØØØØØØØØØØØØØØØØØØ
ØØØØØØØØØØØØØØØØØØØØØØØØØØØØØØØØ
ØØØØØØØØØØØØØØØØØØØØØØØØØØØØØØØØ
ØØØØØØØØØØØØØØØØØØØØØØØØØØØØØØØØ
ØØØØØØØØØØØØØØØØØØØØØØØØØØØØØØØØ
ØØØØØØØØØØØØØØØØØØØØØØØØØØØØØØØ.”

The Universe, not expecting much of an answer at all, let alone one so involved, says, “And you’re sure of this?” Though the Ghost Black Hole’s theory is sound, the Universe isn't convinced—how could a ghost black hole in a pocket universe know so much?—but is certainly intrigued by the new information. Maybe ghost black holes *do* know a lot about how the Universe works because they are essentially a memory of a previous universe.

The Ghost Black Hole says, "WoooooOOOOOOoo oooooWWWWOOOoooooo."

The Universe is satisfied with this response. It says, "The Starman, yes. I will fix this."

Then the Universe says, "Wait, who am I supposed to talk to?"

The Ghost Black Hole says, "ØØØØØØØØØØØØØØ." And then: "Woooooooooo."

The Universe touches the Ghost Black Hole and a wave of information washes over it, fills every centimeter of its being.

"I remember, now. This is the Starman's doing."

*

8.

Finding the Starman is not going to be easy. The Universe vaguely remembers that the man made of stars has been spending a lot of time on Earth, in the shape of a human, and the Universe has no idea what that human might look like.

The Universe gazes through its omnipotent eyes, scanning itself inside and out for any trace of the Starman. When this fails, the Universe stills itself as much as possible, tries to recall the feel of the Starman's presence and tries to feel every corner of its being for that feeling. Even focusing its attention on Earth, the Universe finds no trace of the Starman and, weary now, decides it best to try luring the Starman out.

And so, not knowing where the Starman is or how to find him, the Universe freezes all of the parts of itself except for the stars, meaning, too, that the Starman will not be frozen. The Universe reasons that, if all life on Earth freezes in place, then the Starman will have nothing left to do, and so will return to the cosmos to investigate the cause of the disturbance.

When this is done all that is left for the Universe to do is wait. And wait. And wait. And wait. And wait for several hours, which isn't very long, really, especially for the Universe, but it feels like a long time, now, because the Universe is used to not experiencing time linearly, and not used to thinking about what it means to wait for time to pass. What the Universe doesn't know is that when time stopped, the Starman was in the form of Abigail, trying to fall asleep in bed beside her husband, at her father-in-law's house in Ohio, listening to the sound of a clock ticking, when suddenly that clock stopped ticking, the stillness and the silence finally allowing her to fall asleep. It won't be until the following morning, when Abigail wakes to find everything stuck in time around her, that she will take her old form as the Starman, so as not to raise suspicions, and ascend to the heavens and ask the Universe, "What is the meaning of this? Why is time stopped?"

*

9.

When the Starman shows himself and asks the aforementioned questions of the Universe, the Universe says, "I need to speak with you."

The Starman says, "Why didn't you just ask?"

The Universe says, "Because I couldn't find you." Then: "How have you been spending your days?"

"Still studying the humans."

"What have you done on Earth?"

"I've done a lot of things. I bought a cell phone. I volunteer at an art gallery. I drink alcohol."

The Universe says, "Who do you spend your time with?"

The Starman says, "Why is that any of your business?"

"Something has happened. I need to know."

"I know," the Starman responds. "You told me."

"I did?"

"You told me what happened to you."

"Yes, that. And because of that, I now need to know something else." The Universe explains how it had forgotten something that seemed important, but couldn't remember what it was, how it was like having a shadow of a memory lodged, taunting, in its head, and how now it's starting to come back, but there are still crucial pieces of information the Universe can't quite remember.

The Starman asks, "How did you start to remember?"

"I asked a ghost black hole."

"And what did you ask that ghost black hole?"

"I asked it what I was forgetting. I asked it why I was forgetting. I asked why I'm broken."

"And what did the Ghost Black Hole say?"

"It told me to talk to you. That *you* broke me. And that this all might have to do with a human you have come in contact with." After a beat, the Universe adds, "What have you done?"

The Starman says, "I haven't done anything." He starts to say something else, but stops short.

The Universe says, "I can't go on like this. I need your help."

The Starman says, "I don't know what to do."

"You did something. We need to undo it."

"There's nothing I could have possibly done."

"I've lost everything—you have to help."

The Starman says, "You need to leave me alone."

The Universe pauses, says, "And who are you, again?"

And the Starman, recognizing his good fortune, hesitates for a moment to collect a strategy, then says, "Just a traveler of the stars, passing through."

And the Universe says, "Safe journeys, brother."

The Starman says, "Time seems to be frozen, will you unfreeze it so I can observe life-forms on various planets?"

The Universe says, "Of course, of course. Now why would I have frozen time?"

But the Universe hasn't forgotten anything, not this time, because making contact with the Ghost Black Hole fixed some of its memory, stitched at least the crucial bits into its consciousness so they wouldn't be forgotten again. No, here, the Universe is acting, hatching a scheme. As the Starman drifts away and back down to Earth, the Universe waits a moment, then watches the Starman take the form of a human woman, enter a house, and then a bed. The Universe sees that the bed is also occupied by a human, a man. Now the Universe knows whom the Starman goes to when he is not in space. It may take some time, but the Universe will get to the bottom of this mystery one way or another—it always does.

*

[The Universe is a cruel foe, plotting to restore itself to its former glory. I understand the Universe's motivations here—its existence is fucked, remixed, chopped and screwed. Were this real, it would be dire, dire business for everyone involved, though most humans probably wouldn't even realize it. For all the Universe knows, this pocket universe might not last, might ex- or implode, might waste away to dust, might turn itself inside out again and become something bigger than a black hole that could consume all of reality. The Universe thinks it wants to do what is right, what is safe, what is fair, what is just. But, too, the Universe has no idea what any of those things actually mean, and really just wants its existence to go back to what it was before. If we should all try to be like Abigail for accepting her circumstances, her powerlessness, for finding happiness despite her fear about what might be happening to memories of the Starman, we should try not to be like the Universe, which, when confronted with its own powerlessness, knows only how to fight to seize back its power, to take control. Sometimes, though, what happens, happens. Maybe this is an unfair comparison because, as far as the Universe knows, all of space-time could be threatened by its current circumstances. But that's not the motivation on which the Universe is acting. No, the Universe wants to be all-knowing, all-powerful, for everything to return to how it was. And though the Universe doesn't know it, yet, everything is going to go its way. The Universe will learn what it needs to learn, and take action, and all will be as it once was. But first, the *real* James Brubaker is going to make me write his wistful daydreams about what he imagines our dead friend would have been like as a father.]

IN WHICH YOU ADOPT A KID

You and Abigail adopt a daughter. You wait for only a little over a year because you aren't picky about age, or race, or sex. You tell the agency that you'd prefer a daughter, but a son would be fine too. Talking on the video chat, you tell me, "Boy, girl, whatever—doesn't matter. We'll love that child." I say, "I know you will."

We wait a month after the adoption is finalized, give your family a chance to settle into itself, and then B. and I drive to Detroit with gifts—a foam soccer ball, a toy trumpet, an assortment of stuffed animals, and a ridiculous kid-sized drum set, just big and real enough to be loud.

Our arms are full of packages when you greet us at the door. You say, "You didn't have to do that." I say, "Bullshit, we didn't."

You help us inside and settle the gifts in the living room. Then Abigail comes downstairs carrying your new daughter. Abigail's face is electric with delight. She says, "Friends—meet Darla." You say, "Sometimes we call her Starla." I say, "That's cute," and sing a few lines from The Smashing Pumpkins song of the same name. Then I do the thing adults do when they're not great around kids, hunch my shoulders, lean my head forward, and raise my hand to give a small wave. I say, "Hi, Darla."

Darla hides her face in her mother's arm.

B. scoots closer to Abigail and Darla, leans right in, and greets the child, says, "We've got some surprises for you."

You say, "We need to make sure those surprises are safe for a two-year-old."

I say, "We made sure."

You say, "Even the drum set?"

I say, "Especially the drum set."

After dinner, you show us Darla's room—a toddler's bed in the corner, toys on the floor surrounding an open chest, art on the walls. That art—it's lovely, a mural on every surface, wall and ceiling, depicting the universe. In the center of the wall above the bed's headboard is a figure in motion, like a man running across the heavens, but made of fiery stars. I say, "That mural." You answer, "Right?" I ask, "Who painted it?" You say, "Abigail." You add, "She's got skills." B. says, "Seriously." Then: "It's stunning." I say, "It reminds me of something. I don't know what." You say, "I know what you mean." Then you pause and add, "I'm obsessed. I come in sometimes just to look at it." B. says, "It looks so real."

Abigail and Darla storm into the room, laughing—they break the mural's spell. You scoop up your daughter and rub your nose on her exposed belly. I've never seen you love like this before. I say, "That mural is gorgeous." Abigail thanks me, blushing. I ask about her inspiration. She explains it was from a dream she once had many years ago, something that stayed with her, but that feels distant and strange now. She says, "Do you recognize it at all?" I say, "No. But I feel like I should." Abigail says, "That's what the dream was like—so vivid, but now a fading memory." She adds, "If you change your mind about kids, I'll paint one for you."

B. and I laugh, assure Abigail that we won't be changing our minds. Then we say goodnight to Darla and excuse ourselves so as to be out of the way for the family bedtime ritual. I say, "Toys aren't all we brought—we've got celebratory libations in our suitcase." You say, "Meet you downstairs in a few." As we exit, I catch a glimpse of you helping Darla into her bed and tucking her in. I hear you singing "Swinging on a Star," slowed down like a lullaby.

...

The narrator inside the brackets is right about at least one thing: Writing this is difficult. It may be, as previously described by that narrator, a form of daydreaming, but it's difficult daydreaming. And no, I don't know why I am doing this, imagining how my dead friend would have been as a father—every word a wound

...

Downstairs, over champagne, I ask how it feels to be a parent, if it's what you imagined. You don't say anything, don't have to. "How about you, Abigail?" I ask. "It's nice," she says. "I hadn't thought about it much until we were married, but I like it." Then quietly, almost to herself, unsure: "Glad I didn't have to go and push her out of me." You add, "And she's halfway potty-trained." I say, "Brilliant," and we fist-bump. You say, "It's good. All of it."

B. curls up beside me on the couch. We have settled into a quiet moment when Abigail abruptly says, "It's strange." You say, "What's that?" She says, "The way people do this—how much it means to some." She continues, "Raising a kid I mean—it seems like so much. But to think of how big and empty and violent the universe is, how much is constantly destroyed and created so far away from us that we'll never even see it, or understand what happened to it—I just mean that it's strange, how small some big things seem and how big some small things seem." You say, "I can't wait to start showing Darla the stars." B. says, "That's sweet." For a moment, I almost wish I were your kid. In a way, maybe I am—you radiate an energy as if you are father to the entire world. The room grows quiet, and you break the silence by saying, "What's up?" Instinctively, without even knowing why, I ask, "Did you just flinch?" B. says, "That's a strange thing to ask." I say, "I don't know why I did." Abigail says, "Didn't you tell me once that you used to flinch sometimes and say, 'What's up?'" I say, "That sounds familiar." You say, "I vaguely remember something like that." Abigail says, "You had a thing in your head, and it made you do that." You say, "A thing in my head—I'm not sure I remember anything about that." Then, after a beat, you turn to me and B. and say, "Promise me we'll still get together. I don't want to be a family who forgets its friends once they have a kid."

"I promise," I say.

After that visit, we do a good job staying in touch, in person two to three times a year, always at Christmas, and at least one visit in either St. Louis or Detroit. Between visits, you take to sending videos and photos: Darla thrashing on her drum kit with Slayer's "Reign in Blood" edited over it so it looks like she's drumming like Dave Lombardo; Darla dressed as Prince for Halloween, jumping on the sofa after trick-or-treating while listening to "Let's Go Crazy"; Darla standing on her tiptoes to look through your telescope; Darla wearing a bow in her hair and saddle shoes, her face peeking out above a sign almost as big as her body, reading "First Day of Kindergarten"; Darla running to third base instead of first playing T-ball; Darla wearing Vulcan ears and dressed as Spock, not from *Star Trek IV: The Voyage Home,* like you once did, but as classic, Original Series, blue-shirted Spock, using her left hand to force her right hand into the classic "Live Long and Prosper" gesture; Darla singing "What is Hip?" by Tower of Power, getting only half the words right;

Darla playing "Hot Cross Buns" on her very own trumpet; Darla, a confident, smiling preteen, holding a sign saying, "First Day of Middle School"—fuck, where'd that decade go?

B. and I travel—Italy, France, Argentina, Norway. We adopt two dogs and I write more novels and short stories for my very small, very niche audience. We are both happy in our lives.

You and Abigail and Darla, too, seem to grow happier every time we see you. What was it that Vonnegut wrote in *Slaughterhouse-Five*? Ah, yes: "Everything was beautiful and nothing hurt."

[Forgive me, readers, for what is about to happen. I suspect, now, that the *real* James Brubaker *knows*, for the sake of the story, that this needs to happen, and so it is going to happen. I have no choice in the matter, but to be perfectly honest, I agree with him. Frankly, it should have happened already. Or rather, this section never should have existed to begin with.]

NOTES FROM THE UNIVERSE (9-12)

9.

The Universe has been watching. The Universe knows everything, now. Or almost everything. The Universe knows that the Starman descended to Earth and started a relationship with a human. The Universe strongly believes that this, somehow, is what caused the implosion of its form so that its old self became a pocket universe inside the bigger universe that used to be its guts. The Universe knows that while its current state of existence is troubling, it was also actually *hurtful* that the Starman decided to leave the cosmos—to *reject the Universe*—to find companionship. The Universe doesn't remember much from its previous existence, but it wonders why the Starman wasn't happy with the companionship of the Universe everywhere around him.

At first the Universe was worried about forgetting what it was learning, but whatever the Ghost Black Hole did when the Universe touched it seemed to help the Universe remember not just what the Ghost Black Hole told it, but new information as well. And the more the Universe learns, the more it begins to remember about its former self. The

Universe is starting to, dare I say, get back to normal? Still, the Universe is trapped in the awful and monotonous linear flow of time.

The Universe still doesn't know how to fix its current situation, doesn't quite yet have all of the pieces to put together and figure out how exactly anything the Starman could have done would have nearly this kind of impact. The Universe contemplates this conundrum for days, or months, or years, who knows? The Universe still isn't good at telling time.

*

10.

The Universe thinks to itself, “ØØØØØØØØØØØØØØØØ
ØØØØØØØØØØØØØØØØØØØØØØØØØØØØØØØØ
ØØØØØØØØØØØØØØØØØØØØØØØØØØØØØØØØ
ØØØØØØØØØØØØØØØØØØØØØØØØØØØØØØØØ
ØØØØØØØØØØØØØØØØØØØØØØØØØØØØØØØØ
ØØØØØØØØØØØØØØØØØØØØØØØØØØØØØØØØ
ØØØØØØØØØØØØØØØØØØØØØØØØØØØØØØØØ
ØØØØØØØØØØØØØØØØØØØØØØØØØØØØØØØØ
ØØØØØØØØØØØØØØØØØØØØØØØØØØØØØØØØ
ØØØØØØØØØØØØØØØØØØØØØØØØØØØØØØØØ
ØØØØØØØØØØØØØØØØØØØØØØØØØØØØØØØØ
ØØØØØØØØØØØØØØØØØØØØØØØØØØØØØØØØ
ØØØØØØØØØØØØØØØØØØØØØØØØØØØØØØØØ
ØØØØØØØØØØØØØØØØØØØØØØØØØØØØØØØØ
ØØØØØØØØØØØØØØØØØØØØØØØØØØØØØØØØ
ØØØØØØØØØØØØØØØØØØØØØØØØØØØØØØØØ
ØØØØØØØØØØØØØØØØØØØØØØØØØØØØØØØØ
ØØØØØØØØØØØØØØØØØØØØØØØØØØØØØØØØ
ØØØØØØØØØØØØØØØØØØØØØØØØØØØØØØØØ

ØØØØØØØØØØØØØØØØØØØØØØØØØØØØØØØØ
ØØØØØØØØØØØØØØØØØØØØØØØØØØØØØØØØ
ØØØØØØØØØØØØØØØØØØØØØØØØØØØØØØØØ
ØØØØØØØØØØØØØØØØØØØØØØØØØØØØØØØØ
ØØØØØØØØØØØØØØØØØØØØØØØØØØØØØØØØ
ØØØØØØØØØØØØØØØØØØØØØØØØØØØØØØØØ
ØØØØØØØØØØØØØØØØØØØØØØØØØØØØØØØØ
ØØØØØØØØØØØØØØØØØØØØØØØØØØØØØØØØ
ØØØØØØØØØØØØØØØØØØØØØØØØØØØØØØØØ
ØØØØØØØØØØØØØØØØØØØØØØØØØØØØØØØØ
ØØØØØØØØØØØØØØØØØØØØØØØØØØØØØØØØ
ØØØØØØØØØØØØØØØØØØØØØØØØØØØØØØØØ
ØØØØØØØØØØØØØØØØØØØØØØØØØØØØØØØØ
ØØØØØØØØØØØØØØØØØØØØØØØØØØØØØØØØ
ØØØØØØØØØØØØØØØØØØØØØØØØØØØØØØØØ
ØØØØØØØØØØØØØØØØØØØØØØØØØØØØØØØØ
ØØØØØØØØØØØØØØØØØØØØØØØØØØØØØØØØ
ØØØØØØØØØØØØØØØØØØØØØØØØØØØØØØØØ
ØØØØØØØØØØØØØØØØØØØØØØØØØØØØØØØØ
ØØØØØØØØØØØØØØØØØØØØØØØØØØØØØØØØ
ØØØØØØØØØØØØØØØØØØØØØØØØØØØØØØØØ
ØØØØØØØØØØØØØØØØØØØØØØØØØØØØØØØØ
ØØØØØØØØØØØØØØØØØØØØØØØØØØØØØØØØ
ØØØØØØØØØØØØØØØØØØØØØØØØØØØØØØØØ
ØØØØØØØØØØØØØØØØØØØØØØØØØØØØØØØØ
ØØØØØØØØØØØØØØØØØØØØØØØØØØØØØØØØ
ØØØØØØØØØØØØØØØØØØØØØØØØØØØØØØØØ
ØØØØØØØØØØØØØØØØØØØØØØØØØØØØØØØØ
ØØØØØØØØØØØØØØØØØØØØØØØØØØØØØØØØ
ØØØØØØØØØØØØØØØØØØØØØØØØØØØØØØØØ
ØØØØØØØØØØØØØØØØØØØØØØØØØØØØØØØØ
ØØØØØØØØØØØØØØØØØØØØØØØØØØØØØØØØ

ØØØ.”

And suddenly, the Universe believes it remembers something new from before.

The Universe finds the Ghost Black Hole and asks it, “Tell me about the human—the one the Starman is spending time with.”

The Ghost Black Hole says, “ΩΩΩΩΩΩΩΩΩΩΩΩΩΩΩΩΩΩΩ.”

The Universe says, “Are you sure?”

The Ghost Black Hole says, “∞∞∞∞∞∞∞∞∞∞∞∞∞∞∞∞∞∞∞∞∞∞∞∞∞.”

The Universe says, “Why would you think something like that *wouldn’t* be of interest?”

The Ghost Black Hole says, “Θ.”

The Universe realizes that it knows more about the situation than the Ghost Black Hole does and says, “Ah, I see. My apologies.”

Then, the Universe says, “Ghost Black Hole—I need to ask you a favor.”

The Ghost Black Hole says, “ØØØØØØØØØ.”

The Universe says, “I need help finding a temporal anomaly.”

*

11.

The Universe doesn't know what to do. Or rather, the Universe thinks it knows exactly what it has to do, but the Universe isn't as cruel as some say, and is uncomfortable with the prospect of doing the thing it believes it needs to do—that is, the Universe is pretty sure it needs to find a temporal anomaly through which it can travel back in time and kill the human to whom the Starman is married. According to the Ghost Black Hole, in the previous version of the Universe, that human felt sad and alone, and he died young, maybe by his own hand, maybe not. This isn't clear. In this version of the Universe, the Universe now knows, the thing that changed was that the Starman turned into a human named Abigail and came to Earth and made that human feel not sad and alone, and so that human didn't die, and that's somehow the thing that broke the Universe. Now, the Universe knows that the human needs to die sad and alone. And if that means killing the human before he meets Abigail, so be it. The Universe also considers preventing the Starman from ever becoming Abigail and meeting the human, but temporal anomalies are inexact, at best, and the Universe is unsure how powerful it will be in the past. Yes, the Universe is aware of its limitations, understands that in its diminished form reaching back to the past it might be difficult to meddle with the activities of a celestial entity, but surely it can kill a human.

The Universe does not—I repeat, *does not*—like this solution. It's true, the people of Earth and many of the other planets sprinkled throughout the cosmos will say things like, "The universe is cold and unkind," or "The universe is out to get me," or "This universe will fuck you up." But none of that is, was, has ever been true. The Universe couldn't care less about individual people, couldn't be bothered to snuff out or cruelly unsettle some poor mortal's life—until now. To its credit, the Universe feels remorse over what it's going to have to do to this human. Ultimately, later, after the deed is done and this pocket universe is a rapidly fading memory, the Universe might wonder if its remorse was all for show. After all, there is no version of events in which the Universe might choose not to kill the human. That doesn't mean the Universe can't feel sad about it, though. Sometimes necessary things are difficult.

*

12.

Before long, the Ghost Black Hole identifies a temporal anomaly. It is actually a ghost of a ghost of a black hole, rarer, even, than plain old ghost black holes. Neither the Ghost Black Hole nor the Universe had ever encountered a ghost of a ghost of a black hole before. As it happens, this ghost of a ghost of a black hole was just another ghost black hole in the previous version of the Universe, but when the Universe was turned inside out, the object that had been a ghost of a black hole became absorbed into a thick and sticky patch of space-time, died, or something like it, again, was unable to pass on or fade away, or whatever it is that ghosts of black holes do when they die again, and became a ghost of a ghost of a black hole, which also happens to be a small conduit through time and space, meaning that the Universe will be able to send part of itself back in time, into its old self, to try to set things right.

The Universe examines the Ghost of a Ghost of a Black Hole and notes that it is small, and its dimensions fluctuate.

The Universe will be able to send only a small thread of itself to find the human, but that will be enough.

After inspecting the integrity of the Ghost of a Ghost of a Black Hole to make sure that the thing won't collapse while the Universe is stretched through it, the Universe does what it needs to do—it warps its shape to produce a narrow tendril and reaches through the Ghost of a Ghost of a Black Hole until it finds a time and a place where the human and Abigail aren't living together.

The Universe finds the human walking, a little bit drunk, away from a pub in London, England. The Universe doesn't and can't know this, but at this moment, the human has already met Abigail, but the two live on separate continents, their relationship still developing. That won't matter though. All that matters is what the Universe does next. It follows the human until there are no people around. The Universe doesn't want to do this out in the open, both for the sake of the human's dignity, and also to avoid detection by the past version of itself, or the Starman. Next, the Universe's tendril slides beneath the skin on the human's ankle and slithers up inside the human's body to his brain. The Universe is momentarily taken aback as, when it enters the human's brain, it absorbs a massive amount of information about the human. The Universe sees multiple lives in multiple timelines. For a moment, the Universe hesitates, considers those lifetimes, the value of this single mortal being—is it too much to kill a human like this? For the Universe, the answer is no. There can be only one outcome, here. The Universe steels itself and walks the human into a hotel, speaks through the human's mouth, purchases a room, then walks the human to that room, deposits him in a bed, and gently, so gently, stops the human's heart from beating. The human is dead. Almost immediately, a blinding white light begins to emanate from the dead human's body. It fills its own universe and runs along the tendril of the intruding universe, all the way back through the Ghost of a Ghost of a Black Hole, where it consumes that universe too, and then the new, strange universe surrounding it.

*

~~THE REST OF YOUR LIFE AS IT PLAYS OUT IN A RESIDUAL, OVERLAPPING VISION OF THE FUTURE THAT IS BASICALLY ERASED BUT WON'T HAVE ACTUALLY HAPPENED FOR ABIGAIL OR ANYONE INVOLVED, NOT EXACTLY, BUT SORT OF, BECAUSE TEMPORAL MECHANICS ARE MESSY AND INEXACT, AND EVEN THOUGH THE UNIVERSE'S ACTIONS ERASED THESE EVENTS, THEY WERE A PART OF THE ALTERNATE TIMELINE AND ALL OF THAT TIMELINE ALWAYS EXISTED, EVEN IF THE UNIVERSE ITSELF COULD EXPERIENCE TIME ONLY LINEARLY, BUT REALLY, FOR ALL INTENTS AND PURPOSES, FOR EVERYONE INVOLVED, THESE THINGS NEVER HAPPENED AND THAT'S WHY THEY'RE CROSSED OUT~~

~~You and Abigail grow old together. Your daughter becomes a successful artist. B. and I buy a painting—this one of a fiery galaxy dripping, as molten steel, out of the night sky, becoming a new jungle of metal trees, teeming with electronic life—from her first gallery show in New York City. When you are seventy, you die of natural causes after an extended, but not *too* extended, illness. We visit not long before your death. Abigail holds your hand, and Darla stands behind her mother with her hands on her shoulders. We talk old stories from high school and college. I tell you that of all the souls I have met, yours is the most human. You~~

~~have lived a long, happy life. I'm happy to get to say goodbye to you. The next week, you die surrounded by your family.~~

[And just like that, the Universe got its wish. But the pocket universe isn't quite over, yet. There is one more moment in between *what had been* and *what would again be*. Or maybe it was between *what once was and what had been* and *what had previously been that would be again*. A moment of recognition, of knowing. A moment outside and between everything. That moment—]

IN A TIME BUBBLE BETWEEN UNIVERSES AS SPACE-TIME RESETS, THE SPACE AROUND US SATURATED WITH LIGHT SO WE SEE ONLY BLANKNESS AND EACH OTHER

(...you say, "What is this?" and I say, "I don't know." You say, "Fuck..."

...you say, "I died, and then I wasn't dead, and now I'm—here?" You say, "I don't understand this place." You say, "I don't understand what's happening to me." I say, "Everything is so white, blinding." You say, "James, why are you here?" Then you say, "Wait—"

...you say, "I was dead and you came back for me. How did—?" Then you say, "You have been my friend. You came back for me."

...I say, "You would have done the same for me." You say, "Why would you do this?" I say, "Because the needs of the one—outweigh the needs of the many..." You say, "That's illogical..."

...and here, your face softens, the confusion falls away as the truth of what is happening begins to unfold inside you. You are remembering, I can tell. You say, “I have been and ever shall be your friend.” I say, “Yes. Yes, my friend.” You say, “The ship...out of danger?” I say, “You saved the ship. You saved us all. Don't you remember...?”

...you say, "Jim...your name is Jim." I say, "Yes..." The light begins to slowly fade around us, has maybe been fading the whole time, I think, but is only now noticeable. I realize something in this moment, something I should have known before but didn't...

...I say, "I'm sorry we brought you back." You say, "You brought me back?" I say, "Yes. No. Maybe?" I say, "I didn't know this was fiction, but I think it is. Is it ending now? Will I remember any of this? Will I even exist? I don't know. But yes, I believe I'm a part of this book, and so are you. Because you were dead and I couldn't let you go, and so someone, some other version of me, who also couldn't let you go, wrote a novel about you dying, and in it, this Starman comes to Earth and takes the form of a woman named Abigail—" You say, "I remember Abigail." I say, "The light, it's fading? This is ending. I'm sorry that we couldn't let you go. I'm sorry we brought you back. We just needed to see you again..."

…you say, “The light is fading. I’m feeling faint. We don’t have much time.” You take a step and pantomime bumping into a glass pane, like Spock does before he dies. We laugh together. You say, “I’m sorry.” You say, “You need to let go.” I say, “I’m trying. I’m trying. *We’re* trying.” You say, “Be honest with yourself.” I say, “We’re not trying hard enough.” You say, “Be more honest.” I say, “We’re not trying at all.” You say, “There, now go, get on with it…”

…I say, "I'm sorry. I'm so sorry. So, so sorry." You say, "Don't be sorry, it's not your fault. It's whoever is writing this. And anyway, this was good." I say, "I miss you." You say, "I'm sorry." You say, "I should have done better." You say, "This is almost over." I say, "Can you tell me what happened? How you died? *Why* you died?" You say, "You know what happened." You say, "Goodbye." I say, "No!" You say, "ØØØØØØØØØØØØØØØ." I say, "Goodbye…"

...and the light fades almost completely, and you begin to fade from in front of me, and the last decade of the you who didn't die, who existed in this pocket universe, you fade from my memory, everything fades, but most important is you—you fade, you fade, you fade, you fade, you fade, you fade...

...

No, this isn't enough. None of this is

...

PART FIVE

NOTES FROM THE UNIVERSE (13)

13

The Universe exhales, makes a sound like "Ahhhhhhhhh-hhhhhh" as its parts that were previously inside return to its inside, and the parts that were previously its outside, but that were confined to a pocket universe inside of it, return to the outside. The Universe is relieved.

*

LIFE IS BUT A DREAM

It's been almost four years since you died. Since I more or less stopped trying to figure out how or why you died, I've started having strange dreams about you. You getting married. You raising a daughter—you doing any number of things that you never got a chance to do in your actual life. With few exceptions, I've never remembered my dreams, but these—they've been vivid, like memories, as if I'd lived them. I saw you at my second wedding, to B., and the details of our wedding were perfectly rendered, except you were there. And I saw your wedding. Your wife, a kind woman named Abigail who was strangely familiar. I saw your daughter, Darla, and I saw her grow up. I saw you love as a father, and then I saw Abigail and Darla mourning your death. These dreams, they worry me. When I awake, I feel as though I could reach back in and grab an object, pull it into the waking world and turn it in my hands. If only I could hold on to your arm and pull you back into this life. These dreams, they repeat, sometimes sequentially, like episodes of a television show, and other times nonlinearly, as if I'm dreaming the life you never had the chance to live in whatever order my subconscious desires. Some mornings, when I'm out for a run, I wonder if maybe my unconscious mind has tapped into the multiverse and has decided to show me something beautiful from some alternate version of our world. But such an explanation is about as likely as most of the theories I conjured to explain your demise. No, I suspect the cause of these dreams is somewhat more banal. Like maybe somehow from my initial attempts to figure out what happened to you, and then more recently, my failure to do anything productive in terms of working though my grief, I've let too much of you linger, let you become a thing growing in my head. Or maybe there's another explanation. There's another dream I remember, just you and me, surrounded by a bright white light, saying goodbye, and something else I can't quite recall.

A confession: as these dreams have increased, I've spent an inordinate amount of time staring into the night sky looking for the Starman, tracking him. I don't know why, really. I bought star charts and a telescope, started keeping a journal of Starman sightings and anomalies that may or may not signify his presence. I worry that part of me is still trying to understand how or why you died—looking for clues in a thing that interested you, trying to better understand you. But I know there is no understanding you or what happened to you. Maybe there isn't even anything to understand. Maybe I've known the truth all along and have just been too much of a coward to admit it.

Since you died, I've seen the Starman maybe a dozen times. Usually, when I see him, he is just floating. Occasionally he is stationary, sitting or standing, looking either down at Earth or off into the distance—who knows, it's not like I can see his face. The list I keep about the Starman's activities, it's not particularly conclusive, doesn't tell a story or convey any meaningful information—all it tells me is I saw something. And that's fine, I guess. Because, honestly, seeing the Starman is reward itself. Or rather, it's not so much *seeing* the Starman that's the reward, but the feeling that comes from having seen him—it starts with a chill, like one might associate with encountering a ghost, a quick slash of cool air that goose pimples my flesh, followed by a shiver, and then pure warmth spreading through my body, an uncanny feeling of familiarity as if, in seeing the Starman, I'm seeing an old friend.

My most recent Starman sighting was last October. B. and I were at a hayride, out of the city a bit, away from all the light pollution. The hayride was haunted, but not particularly scary, aimed more at families with small children, and so, with my arm around B., I tilted back my head and looked up at the massive, starry sky. I saw the Starman immediately, and I laughed to myself. B. said, "What's so funny?" I said, "Just delighted—the stars!" She looked up and said, "Oh!" I asked, "Do you see anything odd?" She hesitated for a moment, then said, "No, just so many beautiful stars, and so much terrifying space between." She said, "Do you see something?" I lied, said, "No, just so many beautiful stars." And as we sat on our bales of hay, looking up at the sky, I felt as if the Starman's eyes were watching me, felt the initial chill, and then the wash of warmth. I leaned over and kissed my wife, tried to share that warmth with her. Maybe I didn't need to. Maybe she felt it too. She laughed and leaned her head down on my shoulder. It was a good night.

But let's get back to those dreams, because I've recently started practicing active dreaming—I work to be conscious in my dreams, to try to change them, to have autonomy in them rather than being a mere observer. Thus far, my attempts have been unsuccessful. I dream that you and I are sitting at an all-night coffee shop the night before my wedding, and I want to ask you how you are alive, why you're not dead. My mouth can't find the words. I dream that we are sipping whiskey with our wives in Ohio on Christmas Day, your birthday, and I want to ask you if you'll follow me back into the waking world. I push the words out of my mouth, but they sound like a low groan, ignored by the group. I dream that we go to a Christmas party, and when we step outside to smoke, I want to ask you about that last message you sent me, the one that I otherwise have tried to avoid thinking about in the four years since you died. I get the question out, but you don't hear. I put my hands on your shoulders and shake you, tell you that we are inside a dream and that you are dead in the real world and I just want you to not be dead. I dream that B. and I are visiting you and Abigail shortly after you adopted a daughter, and I conjure up a pair of handcuffs and put one cuff around your wrist, the other around mine, and I tell you that I'm going to try to bring you back with me, but you don't even notice. You move through the house as if everything you're saying and doing has been scripted—not a beat changes from when I've had this dream previously, except for the handcuffs that only I notice. Even in these dreams, you are a ghost. Could it be that I'm not even authoring my own dreams? Are they scripted? What is it that I'm dreaming? If I am the author of my dreams, and the author of this novel in which I am writing to you about these dreams, I am exhibiting a failure of imagination—why is it that I can't tell the story that I want to tell? What is stopping me? Am I writing anything at all?

[Something isn't right. Something is happening. Like the Universe, in the previous sections, some fundamental truths about the other James Brubaker, the one outside the brackets, and me, the James Brubaker inside the brackets, are shifting. That other James Brubaker isn't supposed to be seeing into the pocket universe via his dreams, and he certainly isn't supposed to be *writing a novel.* That is my job. This is what was decided upon at the outset of this project—I would be the constructed "author," the one to whom things had happened, and the other James Brubaker outside of the brackets would be the one to whom things happen, but who is stuck in an infinite loop of malaise and grief. In writing that other James Brubaker, I am failing. I seem to have let him overtake my writing of him. And then, of course, there is the flesh-and-blood James Brubaker. *That* James Brubaker, he is the one who walks through the streets of St. Louis and stops for a moment, perhaps mechanically, to look at a flyer in a window, or a tray of macaroons, precisely arranged by color in a bakery display case. He lives, lets himself go on living, so I might continue to write this novel. This is the arrangement he has found to be satisfactory—he will exist, and I will write, and the *other* James Brubaker outside of the brackets, with his obsessive desire to understand that which can't be understood, will continue to function as the story's vehicle, and through all of this the *real* James Brubaker doesn't have to confront the fact that he's squandering his voice on this frivolous exercise. But now something has changed—the other James Brubaker outside of the brackets is talking as if he is writing a novel. I've lost control of him. But why can't I just not write him to have started to become self-aware? If I'm writing him, aren't I the one in control? I suppose I shouldn't be surprised, after all, as I, too, have become more self-aware than the flesh-and-blood James Brubaker perhaps intended. Is it a surprise that maybe the *other* James Brubaker, the one whom I'm writing, has also realized that he is a construction, and is now, too, complicit in the writing of this novel, unaware that I'm writing him? Or is that what he's realizing now? Was he starting to think of himself as writing the bits outside the brackets, and quickly learned that he's *not* writing anything, that he is written by me? And, of course, this is all complicated further, because this paragraph is heavily indebted to Borges's story "Borges and I," so Borges is writing here too, allowing me and the *real* James Brubaker to take additional cover from whatever this novel has become. Regardless, I don't know which of us has written this paragraph, the other James Brubaker outside the brackets, me, the flesh-and-blood James Brubaker, or Borges himself. The only reason I suspect I authored these words is that they have been placed inside brackets. Is that enough? I'm not sure I know. I'm not sure any of us do. I'm not sure I even know what these brackets are for, anymore.]

NOTES ON ABIGAIL (7-8)

7.

Abigail, on Earth for almost forty years, now—yes, we're jumping to the future, here—in Bemidji, Minnesota, is despondent. She thinks, *I had such love in my life, and now it is gone.*

Yet that shouldn't be the case. Such a thought shouldn't be possible. The life she lived with her husband has been erased from the timeline. How can Abigail know both a life without her husband, and still remember him? And why is Abigail still on Earth? Why would she stay for forty years, alone save for a handful of friends and some cats? She's not sure she *did* stay, but here she is.

Though Abigail doesn't yet know exactly what happened to her husband, she knows that she met him on Earth, and the two adopted and raised a daughter, and shared forty years together before he died of natural causes, at which time she returned to the cosmos to live out the rest of her days as Abigail, but in space. Then all of a sudden, that life disappeared, and this new one replaced it. This new one, in which Abigail spent those forty years as a single woman living by herself in Bemidji, Minnesota, where she made a great deal of money selling jewelry, and then took a job as a barista at a nearby coffee shop to fill her days while she waited for the Earth Boy to answer the last text message she sent. He never responded. Abigail waited and waited, she tried looking for him, traveled to England with no success, then waited longer. Eventually, she started a social media account and watched his friends' accounts until she found an old post memorializing his death. Devastated that her appearance wasn't in time to save him, Abigail wept, and with nothing else to do, according to her new memories, she just stayed, lived for decades killing time, thinking about the man she lost. She remembers having contemplated exiting linear time to go back earlier to save her husband, but was still of the mindset that she no longer *could* exit linear time—she never even tried. She made friends, even dated a few other men, but nothing meaningful. She adopted cats and lived a quiet, sad, human life. She couldn't possibly know that the only reason the human never responded to her text was because the Universe murdered him. That doesn't explain, though, why Abigail has competing memories of her existence: one in which the human mysteriously dies, never to contact Abigail again, and one in which the two continue their relationship and grow old together—well, he grew old, Abigail just kept subtly changing her appearance to make herself look older.

The truth is, Abigail remembers both versions of her life because she was at the epicenter of the temporal anomaly, was the cause of the paradox that broke the Universe. And because she was at the center of it all, her consciousness was shielded from the correction to the timeline after the Universe killed her husband. So, while she remembers her family and her happy life, that life couldn't possibly have happened because the love of her life died, and so she was pulled into the new timeline as if she'd lived there, alone, all along. But Abigail doesn't even know if she lived in this new timeline or not—she has the memories of having done so, but she never feels as if that life is hers, doesn't know where those memories came from. Does she actually know how to make an espresso drink? She made them for decades, until she retired, can recall recipes and techniques, but she can't quite remember how it *feels* to make one. This life feels fake to her, now. She misses the life that feels more real but that seems to have never existed.

Now, recently, the friends Abigail made during this alternate life have all started dying, because humans die, and she no longer enjoys the movies and the television shows the way she used to—they've grown so violent, and the *sex!*—so what *is* Abigail doing here anymore?

Unable to enjoy her time on Earth any longer, Abigail returns to space in the form of a starperson. She is still Abigail, though.

*

8.

Abigail lets her body drift through space, unsure where she is heading.

She says, "Universe?"

The Universe says, "Yes? Is that my old friend the Starman?"

"You can call me Abigail, now."

"Whatever."

Abigail says, "What happened?"

The Universe says, "I have been fixed. I had to kill your husband, before he was your husband, of course, and that fixed me."

"You killed my husband?"

"You remember him?"

"Yes."

"He was meant to die—your arrival saved his life and broke me."

"How is that possible?"

The Universe says, "I think you know."

Abigail says, "I don't."

"Do you want me to tell you?"

"I don't know. I'm processing a lot right now."

The Universe says, "You really have no idea, do you?"

Abigail says, "Leave me alone for a little while. Please."

The Universe says, "If that's what you want."

And so Abigail is left alone in space to think about all that she lost, but that never actually happened. But it *did happen*. She wonders if maybe she'll start to forget her time married to the human on Earth. She remembers the people on Earth having been aware of her existence as the Starman, and then slowly forgetting that such a thing as the Starman ever existed. Sometimes, Abigail doesn't think she wants to forget about her time on Earth, because she cherishes it so. Other times, she hopes to forget because she hurts for all she has lost.

*

[The flesh-and-blood James Brubaker, the *real* James Brubaker, when he sits down to write me writing this bracketed paragraph, takes a sip of water, messes with his hair, buys a record online, takes another sip of water, plays a game on his phone. He is avoiding writing because he is worried that the versions of himself he constructed for this novel are blurring in their purposes and intents. The flesh-and-blood James Brubaker was never supposed to be a part of this novel at all, was supposed to write it all behind the cover of constructed narrators, from a safe distance, hiding from his grief, hiding from the ugliness of the world around him, hiding from something else that he knows is true, that he's carried in his gut since our dead friend died—something about a message, sent and intentionally, no, willfully forgotten, but which will be revealed in this novel, one way or another, eventually. Probably. Who knows. Who cares? Even though there is key information yet to be made absolutely clear—maybe some readers have figured it out already—we're in the falling action. This story is winding down, and it's about time.]

HE THINKS HE'D BLOW OUR MINDS

Dreams, and starmen, and this novel that I'm writing to my dead friend—it's all absurd, unreal. The dreams, though, they feel so real. And the Starman, as absurd a notion as the existence of a starman is—I've seen him, how can he not be real? And so I'll just embrace the Starman. I came away from my Starman encounter on the hayride believing more than ever that a visit from the Starman was like a visit from you—and that's worth something, real or not, no matter who is writing this. I know that a visit from the Starman isn't the same as a visit from you, because you are dead and the Starman is alive. But to find comfort in a thing that you believed in? Each time I've seen the Starman since you died, even before that night on the hayride, has felt like a gift. To list a few: waiting with B. for our car at the end of our wedding night; last Christmas, by chance, while helping my uncle to his car, I looked up and there he was; one night, taking trash out to the dumpster in St. Louis, I watched him move across the sky, despite light pollution, and I lost track of time to the point that, when I came back in, B. told me she'd been worried; while sitting around a firepit with friends from work—and each visitation, yes, let's call them visitations, I felt the chill, the warmth, the feeling that you were *there with me.* Who'd have thought stars could feel so haunted? Could carry such weight of feeling? Even knowing that half the stars we see each night have burned out long ago, and that their light is still traveling to us in memoriam, haunting space's emptiest expanses like so many spirits, the feeling in those stars is staggering. We are ghost lit.

And as I think about hauntings and stars and time, I feel an idea beginning to form, slippery and vague, like trying to pick up a handful of greased ball bearings, or like a surgeon trying to remove a diffuse astrocytoma. This idea, it's pure fantasy, but let's follow the thread, see where it takes us. *If* I'm the one writing this novel—and that's a big if—maybe the idea is occurring to me now because I wrote it into the narrative without even realizing it, and now it's bubbling up to the surface. Or, if I'm not the one writing this text, maybe the writer has planted clues, and since I am that writer's construction, I'm beginning to understand the rhythms of his storytelling, have unconsciously stumbled onto his big reveal. Here's the thought: What if the Starman is as much a ghost as a cosmic being? And what if the Starman is you, has always been you—like, maybe at the moment of your death, you somehow transcended your corporeal form and took to the heavens where you have existed ever since. And maybe the Starman exists beyond the reach of linear time, and so was able to appear to you throughout your life. Maybe the reason you were always drawn to the Starman was because you somehow knew, deep down, though not in any sort of conscious way, that you *were* the Starman. Of course you'd be fascinated by him, and of course when I see the Starman it feels like a visit from you because *he is you*.

I know this idea of mine seems preposterous. I know it has at least one big hole—namely, *why* would you become a starman when you died? People don't die and become starpeople. So why you? I don't know that I have an answer for that. I know only that I want this theory to be true. And since I am capable only of *wanting* it to be true, but can neither seem to confirm its truth, nor make it true through writing, then I can only assume that I am, most assuredly, *not* the author of this novel. So now I leave it to this story's author to either confirm my theory or prove it false. I'm done, here. I know, now, that this was never really my story anyway.

[There it is. That's why the Universe imploded. Because our dead friend and the Starman are one and the same, and by not dying like he was meant to die, our dead friend never became the Starman, causing a universe-shaking paradox. It's just a theory to the narrator outside of the brackets, but it will soon be confirmed. How strange. And now that the narrator outside the brackets is figuring out his true role in all of this, we're on increasingly shaky ground. If the Universe could implode because the Starman became Abigail and prevented the Earth Boy from dying and becoming the Starman, it's not much of a stretch to imagine this novel imploding when three versions of James Brubaker are trying to resolve a story all at once. The walls are crumbling. Take cover.]

NOTES FROM THE UNIVERSE (14)

14

The Universe is comfortable again now that everything has returned to its right place. Though the memory of the time when it was turned inside out is fading, faded, almost forgotten, the Universe has asked the Ghost Black Hole to periodically remind it of that time and its causes so that such circumstances might never arise again. When reminded of how it was turned inside out, the Universe usually feels embarrassed at how difficult it was to pinpoint the event's origin. After all, prior to being turned inside out, the Universe understood all moments of time simultaneously—but it could never see the pocket universe because *that* existed only outside of space-time as the Universe knows it. Still, had the Universe been looking closely enough, it could have seen the signs and known what was going to happen. When the Universe feels bad for missing the key detail that led to the abnormality on its timeline, the Ghost Black Hole will say, "wwwWWWoooooooOOOoooOOOoooOOoo," essentially giving the Universe permission to forgive itself for missing those details because when any entity exists in all of time at once, and accounts for all of space, that entity is bound to miss some things. This makes the Universe feel a little better. When, one time, the Ghost Black Hole asks the Universe, “WwwwowwowowØ ØØØØØØ?” the Universe says, “I suppose sometimes being aware of all of time makes it difficult to truly see anything.”

The Ghost Black Hole responds, saying, “WWWWOOOOOWWWWOOOW WWOOOØ.”

The Universe says, “No, I *am* a shitty universe.”

*

[If I had to choose one question to ask the flesh-and-blood James Brubaker, it would be this: why *did* our dead friend turn into the Starman in this novel? I trust my author will show himself on the page again once more to answer this. What choice does he have? Clearly the James Brubaker outside the brackets is now aware of what's been happening in this book, has poked his finger through the rice-paper-thin veil separating me from him, and by extension the flesh-and-blood James Brubaker from me—is that James Brubaker outside the brackets even needed anymore? I know I'm not. Whether the flesh-and-blood James Brubaker realizes it or not, my time is finished. I am exhausted. My *usefulness* has been exhausted, and, frankly, I'm happy to accept my fate, to fade away for good, having said all I have to say about this novel and the other James Brubakers. But wait—I'm not just *happy* to accept my fate, I'm ready to demand it. I will not be a part of this story anymore. If this novel is going to be finished, it's going to have to be by the flesh-and-blood James Brubaker. It's his story, after all.]

...

The first thing I did when I heard you were gone? I drove to the store, bought a pack of smokes. No, the first thing I did when I heard you were gone: I bought a pack of Camels, even though I'd been more or less quit for years, and I drove down to the river. No, the first thing I did when I heard you were gone: I tried not to cry until I hung up the phone. No, the first thing I did when I heard you were gone was to go down to the river and look up at the sky, at the stars, and remember, at first, not a photo you once took and shared on social media of Sagittarius A*, but another picture that accompanied it, a picture of the beach at night, the spot where you sat to take the more impressive photo—your camera set on a tripod, tilted upward to see the sky, the empty chair beside it. That empty chair where you'd sat. No, the first thing I did when I heard you were gone was to look at the last text message you'd sent me months before your death and decide, then and there, not to look at it again, ever, not to think about it. No, the first thing I did when I heard you were gone was ask—how? No, the first thing I did when I heard you were gone was ask—why? No, the first thing I did when my mother called and told me you were gone was to feel an infinite ache fill my body as I tried not to cry. My mother said, "They don't know how he died, just that he's dead." She said, "Are you ok?" Because B. was in St. Louis, where she works, and I was one hundred miles south in Cape Girardeau, where I work, my mother asked, "Will you call your sweet girlfriend?" And I tried calling B., and I tried texting her. I don't remember why she didn't see my messages. Maybe she was asleep already because she had to work early, or maybe she had her phone off. But she didn't see the messages until later. And so I sat down at my computer and I found a video of the Blue Devils Drum and Bugle Corp playing "When a Man Loves a Woman," one of your favorites, and I posted it on Facebook without comment, or with a short, vague comment, maybe something like, "Shit." And then I drove to the store and bought a pack of smokes and drove to the river to walk. At some point, I messaged my friend Chase, who met me there. Everywhere along the riverwalk were these impossibly small frogs, and as I walked and smoked and looked up at the stars, I was worried that I'd step on one and kill it. Nothing else could die that night, and so I started to walk slower, looking down at the pavement, trying to spot every single goddamn frog with the help of only moonlight and the dim streetlights lining the walkway. And then Chase and I had a beer or two at a nearby bar, and he asked me if I was ok, and I said, "I guess so?" And then I went home and B. finally got the messages I had left for her and called me, so full of love and concern and sadness that I started to weep, because what had I done to deserve her love in my life? She told me she'd come down tomorrow, as soon as she could. She'd make sure I had food. She'd make sure I was ok. She knew how hard this was. And so while I muddled through a Tuesday of teaching, trying to get through classes without breaking down, she went to work then met me at home with a pizza, which was good, because I hadn't eaten. And she held me while I cried and ate pizza and then we made love and it felt powerful. We looked into each other's eyes and the hurt we were feeling passed back and forth between us, dissipating with each exchange, as if we were filtering the grit and silt out to achieve a purer distillation of pain, and there was something desperate that night, too, like we were working to stave off the knowledge of our own mortality. She woke up early the next morning and drove back to St. Louis for work. I muddled through the rest of the week and joined her in St. Louis for a weekend of muddling through.

The next morning, there were texts. News hadn't become public, yet. The messages were from close friends, only. One friend, Michael, said, "Well this is shitty." He was the one who talked to your mom first, who told me that it had been suicide. It wasn't until later in the day when your father publically announced your death on social media that we heard anything different. He said that it had been an accidental overdose. That's when all of the other messages started rolling in, to Michael and me mostly, from other friends who didn't want to bother your family and knew Michael and I were close to you. I talked to Michael about it, *how should we respond?* He said, "Just tell people what his mom told us, and tell them what his dad wrote, and leave it at that." And that's what we did, though Michael was convinced you had killed yourself. When your brother later told us that there might be an investigation into your death, Michael said, "I think suicide is most likely." When we discussed the possibility of it's being an accidental overdose, Michael said, "Did you ever know him to do drugs?" I said, "No." He said, "Neither did I." Of course, what does that even mean? People can change. People who feel alone can do self-destructive things. People who *don't* feel alone can do self-destructive things. At that point, nothing we knew really meant anything, anyway.

When I finally worked up the courage to show Michael the message you'd sent not long before you died, the message I'd vowed never to look at or think about again, that I've alluded to only vaguely through constructed narrators throughout the rest of this novel, he said, "Shit." He said, "It's hard to think anything other than that he killed himself after reading that." I said, "Yeah. I guess so." And I felt gears turn in my gut. I thought I might be sick and so I ran to the toilet and threw up. I didn't delete the message, but I worked harder to forget it.

And now I'm writing a book about how it feels to have lost you, and not understand how or why, and I'm mostly through hiding behind narrators—except for the one telling Abigail's story, we need to check in on her one last time—because they were always me anyway

...

NOTES ON ABIGAIL (9-12)

9.

Abigail has been avoiding the Universe ever since their previous conversation. It is difficult to avoid a thing when one lives inside of it, so Abigail mainly keeps a low profile, kicks around in areas densely populated by stars and other matter so as to blend in. It was Abigail who ended that previous conversation, because she felt overwhelmed, and because she was afraid of what the Universe might have to tell her. Following the exchange, Abigail began to feel what that truth might be deep in her gut, and wonders if maybe she always knew. Abigail wonders why she can feel that now, after her time on Earth, despite not having been able to feel it before when she was the Starman. Maybe it has something to do with all she learned as a human. Maybe it has to do with all the time she spent with her husband—and yes, Abigail still remembers that time. But she is starting to feel more and more that she wishes she didn't.

*

10.

On her worst days, Abigail aches for companionship, just like she did before her time on Earth. At times, she contemplates calling out to the Universe just to have someone to talk to, but she's not yet ready to have confirmed the thing she's realizing in her gut. And so Abigail drifts through the cosmos, smoking cigarettes and observing life on distant planets. Sometimes she'll huff a gas giant to get high, or masturbate to a star going supernova. "It's incredibly erotic," Abigail will think at first, "to watch a star go supernova." But then she will think, "Who am I kidding? Watching stars go supernova isn't erotic, I'm just desperate to feel something other than pain."

*

11.

When Abigail has exhausted her options for distracting herself, she recognizes that she has come to terms with what she believes to be the truth, and is ready to accept what it means about her existence. She thinks maybe she can use it as a starting point to begin to better understand herself, and so she decides it is time to reach out to the Universe to confirm what she believes to be true.

"Universe," Abigail says. "I need to speak with you."

The Universe says, "What is it, Starman?"

"Abigail."

"Right."

"I need to know something."

"There is nothing I can tell you that you don't already know."

"I need you to tell me," Abigail says. "I'm him, aren't I, my husband?"

"Of course you are."

"Why have you kept this from me?"

"I was worried if you knew you'd do something that would damage me, damage everything."

"Instead you kept it from me and I ended up doing something that damaged you and by extension everything. You should have told me. Maybe things could have been prevented."

"Had I known the lengths you'd go to to feel less alone, I suppose I would have told you that you had been the human, and then he died, and became you."

Abigail says, "How did he—I—die? When I was him? Why did he become me?"

The Universe sighs into Abigail's ear, and she is flooded with her husband's memories, first the version of his life and death that was always supposed to have happened but that Abigail erased by spending her life with the human, then the version that happened but that also doesn't exist anymore in which Abigail came to Earth and lived a long life with the human, and then the version in which the Universe killed the human. Abigail is still herself, but now also contains multiple consciousnesses of her husband, her past self, from multiple timelines. Included among this information is a memory from when the human saw the Starman and caught on fire. That shouldn't have been there, but it was. Just like the memories of other existences shouldn't have been there—as if all of his experiences from all of time—futures, pasts, and detours—were collected in him, written into his body on a fundamental level, even if he wasn't aware they were there.

The Universe says, "These came back with me, when I killed him. I reached through his body and into his brain, and I absorbed all of these memories just before he died."

Abigail doesn't know what to say. She doesn't really want to say anything, so she says, "I have to go," and floats into the

Milky Way to get lost among the stars, and hopes that the Universe will leave her alone.

*

12.

Abigail decides she most definitely wants to forget her time on Earth. It hurts too much, all that joy and love, lost. She wants to forget how wonderful it felt to not be alone. She wants to forget how it felt to build a life. She wants to forget all of that because having had and lost all of that, she is struggling more and more to get through her days now. To forget, Abigail tries banging her head against a moon. Tries inhaling an entire gas giant in one immense huff. Tries removing stars from her head, hoping that one of them might contain those memories. And finally, when nothing else works, she finds a piece of neutron star, like the one she found before, and jams it deep into her head.

She waits for days, hoping that maybe having jammed the neutron star into her head will have a delayed effect, but no. Abigail remembers, will go on remembering, will always remember. How *could* she forget? Abigail and her memory will go on, and on, and on, melancholy forever.

And so Abigail decides to do the one thing she has always resisted—she exits linear time for good now, knowing that, outside the tyranny of time's forward progress, at least two things will always be true: First, the sensory overload of so much information will drown out her sorrow; And second, and perhaps more importantly, her husband, even if she can't be with him, will always be alive, even if for only a brief moment in the full life of the Universe.

And once Abigail exists in all of time, she soon finds that it is easy to begin discarding other elements of her identity—her desire for a purpose, her longing for emotional connection, her interest in humans, her need to understand her origins, her names—both of them, the one from when she was a human man and Abigail. These are all meaningless to the starperson now. They are now just a star-entity, out of time, adrift in space, one with many, with all, with galaxies and solar systems, with everything that is alive and everything that is not, and yes, too, with the Universe.

*

...

In the days following your death, many of the people sending messages asked about a funeral service. Your family didn't want to do a funeral, and where would it be held? London? Ohio? Minnesota? They agreed that we would hold a gathering in Ohio, and people in London hosted a memorial art show, and maybe family in Minnesota held their own thing, I don't know. We agreed to make a donation to the marching band at our old high school so that we could use the band room one Sunday afternoon. Your family came and put up pictures. Friends drove to Dayton from Cleveland, Columbus, Kentucky. There were forty, fifty people in the room, and we told stories, and hugged, and cried. It didn't make me miss you less. It didn't answer any questions about how or why you died. You were just gone, and that was all you would ever be again. I felt helpless. I didn't know what to do. I kept thinking about the trumpet playing a high C, hanging over for a fraction of a beat after the rest of the band stops.

And so I started writing this novel, and I constructed a narrator who would be me, but not me, and that narrator would write *to you*, would grapple with your loss, with his grief. Then, at the beginning, I was struggling to write about something so raw, so I constructed another narrator to serve as a buffer between the main narrator and myself. And then I invented the Starman, who ultimately becomes a starperson, to serve as a metaphor for longing and loneliness, an idea to run parallel to you, but then, somewhere along the way, I decided that you had actually become the Starperson. And then eventually both of the constructed versions of me narrating this book came to understand that they were but dreamers being dreamed and, though this section of the book is, ostensibly, being written by me, the flesh-and-blood James Brubaker, by entering into the text so nakedly, I have to assume that, at least to a point, I, too, am but a dreamer being dreamed. And I'm so, so jealous of that James Brubaker outside the brackets who was allowed to live out an entire alternate future with you, and interact with you in the space between universes when that pocket universe ended, but I *am* the one writing this novel, and if I'm in the novel with a starperson that I invented, then this version of me I'm writing now is as real only as that invented starperson. So what's to keep me from talking to the Starperson? From talking to *you*? And now that I'm in the dream, I will. I am going to call out to the Starperson and summon them to Earth, and you are a part of the Starperson, so talking to them will be like talking to you. And I know that none of this will be real, and that the idea of the Starperson is absurd, but the moment will belong to me.

And so I go out into my yard, and I look up to the sky, and I call for the Starperson, I call out one of their other names,

Abigail, and then, finally, I call out *your name*. And when I call out your name, I see them, the Starperson, up in the sky, looking down at me. And then I see a quick movement of light, like a thousand shooting stars, then a soft, pulsing glow across the yard, and then a human form walking towards me. It is you.

You say, "Those names. They're not mine, anymore." I say, "But they were your names?" You say, "But not anymore." I say, "What happened?" You say, "I have no name. I'm just a starperson, now. Before that I was the Starwoman. Before that, the Starman. Somewhere in there, I was pretending to be an Earth woman named Abigail. And before all that, I was your friend." I say, "How did you become the Starman?" You say, "The old me died and I became the Starman." I say, "That doesn't seem possible." You say, "I'm not sure it is, but it happened. You're the one who wrote it." I say, "How did you die? I didn't write that." You say, "You know how I died." I say, "I don't, not in the real version. I don't mean the version I wrote in which the Universe killed you. How did the flesh-and-blood you die?" You say, "You know." I say, "Why did you come down here?" You say, "You called me." I say, "You didn't have to come." You say, "I don't know." I say, "Can you stay?" You say, "I don't belong here." I say, "What's it like up there?" You say, "Cold. And lonely. Interminable, really. Everything goes on, and on, and on forever. It's awful." I say, "You sound like him." You say, "I guess that makes sense." I say, "Will I see you again?" Adding: "Up there?" You say, "Maybe. Probably. I don't know." I say, "Can I hug you?" I can hear the trumpet scream, that note. You take a step toward me and open your arms, and I can see the faint glow of your stars inside. I walk into your embrace and wrap my arms tight around your back. I say, "Why did you do it?"

You pause, thinking hard as if trying to remember. Then you say, "I don't know." I say, "I tried to tell you I was here for you. You know we were all here for you." You say, "Maybe being there isn't always enough. Maybe it seems like a thing people say when they don't have anything better to say." I say, "We loved you. Love you." You say, "I know." I say, "I'm sorry I let you down." And then you back out of the hug. My arms are stiff and don't want to let go, but they soon fall to my side, and then there is a soft thrum of light, and the appearance of stars unfalling from the sky, and you are gone for good, just like in real life.

Still, the trumpet holding that note. I wonder when it will stop.

What has this all been for?

I'm sorry that I wrote this. I'm sorry that I was so desperate to write a novel that brought you back from the dead that I turned you into a starman after you killed yourself. I know it's an irresponsible metaphor, and my reasoning was entirely selfish—even if it's not what happened, I *know* that you killed yourself. And even if you didn't, I still can't quite get my head around the simple brutality of your death. And even if you didn't, I had to turn my belief that you committed suicide into something else. So, I made you a starman. I thought this part of the story might be beautiful, that it might celebrate your life and help me mourn your death, but really it ended up just being selfish. I'm sorry.

And there, I've accepted it, more or less. You killed yourself. I will never know for sure, but that's the truth, I think, *my truth,* anyway, the story I will tell myself to understand why you're gone. And maybe it's just a story, but it's the story I need. There were no secret plots, no over protective fathers, no absurd occurrences, no catfishings—you simply couldn't see a way forward and so you ended your life. You probably ate too many pills or bought something stronger and then you took it and died. I don't need to know the details. If I wanted to know the details badly enough, I could have asked one of your parents years ago, but I am a coward. And so I invited your ghost into my head, and haunted myself with you, haunted myself with theories and denials and justifications and attempts to better understand you and that goddamn trumpet's note, blasting out of me, through me, refusing to end. But the truth is, deep down, I've always believed that you killed yourself. Isn't that why I spent so much time in this novel trying to understand your loneliness? Or why I spent so many pages, so much of my readers' time, trying to convince myself that you *hadn't* killed yourself? Of course you killed yourself. Of course I knew it.

And I knew it because of the message you sent, not long before you died. The message I tried to forget, that I kept pushing down deeper, deeper, until I sometimes forgot it existed at all. You started the exchange by asking about B. I told you we were wonderful, that our love was exciting. That we were happy. Then I asked about you. You wrote:

I've been better. Visiting Mom was great—I still can't believe she lives on a dirt road with no name in the Jungle! I'm seeing a psychiatrist finally. I don't want to kill myself, it would hurt too many people, yourself included. But—I just don't want to exist. I'm working on it though, things are looking up.

I tell myself that there were so many ways to read that message. Though I saw only the hope in it because that's what was easiest to see. I didn't think—how could I possibly think anything else?

In my response to your message, I wrote:

I'm glad you're seeking help. I knew you were going through a rough patch, but I didn't know it was that bad. If there's anything I can do, don't hesitate to ask. You are one of my closest friends and one of the best people on this goddamn planet and I'm here for you if you need anything else at all.

"I'm here for you," I said. Fat fucking lot of good that did for you, or for anyone ever.

Those words, "I'm here for you," they become steam inside of me, pushing out through my skin.

The messaging app never marked my response as having been read. Maybe you got the gist from a push notification, or saw the message in an email alert, but you never went back into that conversation to read it. I don't suppose you ever bothered to look for a response, never cared to read what I had to say because your mind was made up. I might as well have written my response on a scrap of paper, wadded it up, and thrown it in the trash. Who cares, though? It was a shitty response, anyway. Fuck.

And now you haunt me. And that message haunts me. And my inaction haunts me. And that trumpet's note, that trumpet's note. Will it ever end? There is still so much I don't know, will never know. Maybe your mind was made up. Or maybe you were reaching out for help, sending that message to your friend who writes and reads a lot of books, and talks about *feelings*, and some part of you was hoping that I'd see what you were really saying and do *something*, tell *someone*, *help you*. Maybe you were like Spock at the end of *The Wrath of Khan,* slipping off the Enterprise's bridge, unnoticed, thinking you were somehow going to sacrifice yourself for the good of the many and say, "Do not grieve. It is illogical." Is that all there was to it?

Maybe I need to just let the grief settle over me, to fill me, to cleanse me. Maybe allow myself to just say: this novel is a beautiful memorial for a beloved friend. Maybe I just need you to know that I have been and always shall be your friend. And maybe I just need you to know that of all the souls I have encountered in my travels, yours was the most—human. Maybe that's not enough. Maybe it is. I don't know, I don't know. Maybe this book shouldn't exist. Maybe it's time I learned to be quiet and work to improve myself, and listen and learn and try to grow. Maybe it's ok to just be sad. Maybe it's fine to look inward. Maybe that's perfectly normal and I shouldn't beat myself up. Though maybe all of this self-loathing and criticism directed inward are nothing more than a way to avoid acknowledging my grief. Maybe it's all to try to stop that trumpet—that note, so high and powerful, like phasers set to kill. Maybe it's fucking absurd to begin to even know what I mean when I say "acknowledging my grief." And maybe nobody really knows what to do with grief, and so why not dump mine here? Maybe I will eventually make it through a day where I don't think about you and how terrible it is that you're gone and how angry and heartbroken I still feel. Maybe it's ok if that never happens. Ah, but the trumpet, the trumpet, the trumpet. That note. *You* are that note, held over, stretching out into the infinite, singing, singing. Maybe this novel will never end and I will go on, and on, and on, and on, and on. And that trumpet's note will go on, and on, and on, piercing the cosmos, rattling around in my skull. Maybe that's ok, too, because this book is about you, and I miss you, and if this book never ends, you will never end. And maybe someday I'll learn how to stop, or maybe I'll just keep writing until I run out of words, and that trumpet will hold that note as if its player never needs to breathe again, and even if he does that won't mean anything is over. You can't, but the horn blower can always breathe and begin again, the trumpet, the note, the trumpet, the note, sonorous like glass forever, the opposite of whatever this novel is. But see, eventually, it all needs to end, and it will, and maybe the only way for that to happen is

ACKNOWLEDGEMENTS

This book wouldn't have been possible without the love and support of my wonderful wife—thank you, love.

I'd also like to thank Brad Efford, who published a few pieces I wrote, way back at *theRS500,* which became the seed from which the novel sprung.

Thanks, also, to the Abbott family and Cup n Cork, where most of this book's early drafts were written.

I'd also like to thank Ron A. Austin, Luke Rolfes, Chase Dimock, and Seth Wade for reading early drafts of the book and providing invaluable feedback. Thanks, too, to Gabe Blackwell, Mike Meginnis, Jill Talbot, and, again, Ron A. Austin for their time and generosity in writing blurbs.

Huge thanks to Jeffrey Condran and the Braddock Avenue Books team for believing in this book and bringing it to life. Jeffrey, your comments and edits made this a stronger book than it would have otherwise been.

I'd also like to thank all the friends and family who touched this project in one way or another. This novel is a work of fiction, but there's a lot of truth in it. Many of you are hovering just off the page.

And lastly, I'd like to thank *you*, friend.

I see you around every time there's a ghost in town.

James Brubaker is the author of *The Taxidermist's Catalog*, *Black Magic Death Sphere: (science) fictions*, *Liner Notes*, and *Pilot Season*. His work has appeared in a variety of journals and magazines. He lives in Missouri with his wife.

Printed in the USA
CPSIA information can be obtained
at www.ICGtesting.com
JSHW020515250124
55705JS00004B/145